# The Cyborg

First published in Italian as
*Il Cyborg: Saggio sull'uomo artificiale*
© ShaKe Edizioni, Milano, ed eredi Antonio Caronia


**Bibliographical Information of the
German National Library**

The German National Library lists this publication in the Deutsche
Nationalbibliografie (German National Bibliography); detailed biblio-
graphic information is available online at http://dnb.d-nb.de.


Published 2015 by meson press, Hybrid Publishing Lab,
Centre for Digital Cultures, Leuphana University of Lüneburg
www.meson-press.com

Design concept: Torsten Köchlin, Silke Krieg
Coverimage: Michael Deistler (courtesy of Dorothea Schlueter, Galerie)
Printed in Germany by Schaltungsdienst Lange oHG, Berlin


ISBN (Print):    978-3-95796-010-8
ISBN (PDF):      978-3-95796-011-5
ISBN (EPUB):     978-3-95796-012-2
DOI:             10.14619/007


The digital editions of this publication can be downloaded freely at:
www.meson-press.com.


Funded by the EU major project Innovation Incubator Lüneburg

# The Cyborg:
# A Treatise on the Artificial Man

**Antonio Caronia**

Translated by
**Robert Booth**

With a preface by
**Tatiana Bazzichelli**

**meson press**

Antonio Caronia (1944–2013) studied mathematics, logic,
and linguistics at the University of Genova, finishing it with
a thesis on Noam Chomsky. Besides his studies he was a
political activist in the Italian radical left. Further fields
in which he conducted research were the study of mass
culture, especially the interrelation of science, technology,
and imagination. In addition, he turned to philosophy and
anthropology, most notably concerning science fiction,
comics, digital images, virtual reality, and telematic networks. Caronia worked as a translator, journalist, and
university teacher. He taught at the Academy of Fine Arts of
Brera (Milano), at the New Academy of Fine Arts (NABA) of
Milano, and was the Director of Studies of M-Node, linked to
the Planetary Collegium directed by Roy Ascott in Plymouth,
UK.

# Contents

# Preface to the English Edition

Tatiana Bazzichelli

Since its first publication in 1985, *The Cyborg* has gone through several iterations. Antonio Caronia himself wrote a first preface for the second edition in 2001 and another one for the third in 2008 (both published by ShaKe Editions), which is translated and included in this book. In both his prefaces, Caronia points out that *The Cyborg* is written to belong, more than to the author, to the readers themselves, who are invited to embody and collectivize his theoretical reflections covering a period of more than twenty years. According to Antonio Caronia, this means that readers should feel free to bend the book's meaning, start new paths of theory and practice that are not necessarily the ones imagined by the author, and most of all, use his reflections as a tool of criticism and action able to expand into other unpredictable layers of understanding and intervention.

The author left us in January 2013, unfortunately too early to see the international edition of *The Cyborg* published and made available to a wider audience. Writing this preface, I will follow a "situated perspective," as Antonio would probably suggest, drawing upon Donna Haraway's concept of *situated knowledges* to contextualize his book for an international public.[1] Here, I will assume an Italian researcher's point of view on hacktivism and network culture, having lived in northern Europe for some years, and having been a colleague and friend of the author in various

1    The essay, "A Cyborg Manifesto: Science, Technology, and Socialist-Feminism in the Late Twentieth Century," by Donna Haraway, first published in *Socialist Review,* no. 80 (1985): 65–108, and later in her book *Simians, Cyborgs and Women: The Reinvention of Nature* (New York: Routledge, 1991), deeply inspired the reflections of Caronia on the contamination between the body and the machine, and on the need to assume an intellectually situated perspective.

intellectual and political adventures around the network of AHA: Activism-Hacking-Artivism.[2]

Following another of Caronia's suggestions, we should read this book keeping in mind its use as a possible "tool for collective fights", to uncover theoretical and practical territories as yet unimagined. This approach is one of the things I remember most strongly from my conversations with Caronia, who was a polyphonic person able to generate sparks in your mind, by being very intellectually acute, precise, innovative and quite direct and critical when necessary.

Caronia's writings reflect his diverse experiences in many fields of study and action: with a university background in mathematics, and a final dissertation on Noam Chomsky, for most of his life Antonio Caronia studied philosophy, anthropology and linguistics; he was politically active in the Italian grassroots movement since the seventies, initially as part of the collective *Un'ambigua utopia* (An Ambiguous Utopia), named after the subtitle of *The Dispossessed*, the science fiction novel by Ursula K. Le Guin (1974); he was also an expert in digital culture, media aesthetics, science fiction, and virtual reality since its early phase; a Professor of Communication Studies at the Brera Academy of Fine Art, and the Research Director of the Ph.D Planetary Collegium M-Node, affiliated to the University of Plymouth, based at NABA, the New Academy of Fine Arts in Milan, where he taught Aesthetics of Media, and Digital Cultures; he was also a writer, journalist and professional English-Italian translator, overseeing the Italian editions of books by James G. Ballard and Philip K. Dick.[3]

---

2    *AHA: Activism-Hacking-Artivism* is the project on hacktivism and net culture in Italy that I started in 2001, and a community around the aha@ecn.org mailing list which is still active today (http://lists.ecn.org/mailman/listinfo/aha).

3    In addition, together with Domenico Gallo, who was also a member of the Ambiguous Utopia collective, Antonio Caronia co-wrote the book *Philip K. Dick: La macchina della paranoia – Enciclopedia Dickiana* (Milan: Agenzia X,

Since Antonio Caronia worked on *The Cyborg* for quite some time, personally editing its various editions, this publication should be considered not only as a way of following his theoretical path, but also as a means to get closer to his perspective in the development of critical media and political practices in Italy. This book is part of a puzzle that is probably only possible to solve by reading other works by the same author, and by the network around him, but *The Cyborg* is certainly crucial to a specific phase in the development of digital culture from the eighties until today, not only in Italy, but internationally. *The Cyborg* is a complex book, not because of the language used by the author, which is quite accessible, but because it needs to be understood as a metaphor of *the possible*, a reflection on the development of an emerging imaginary in Italian society, politics and culture, that refers to personal experiences of the author covering almost thirty years, which he shared with a wide network of people, in the city of Milan and beyond.

One of Antonio Caronia's great contributions was to introduce Italian readers to writers like Philip K. Dick, James G. Ballard, and William Burroughs, and to provide a critique of the works of science fiction authors from the early thirties and forties such as Edmond Hamilton and Catherine L. Moore, from the sixties and seventies such as Samuel R. Delany, and to facilitate a critical understanding of many other writers within the context of the cyberpunk literature of the eighties. But most of all, the peculiarity of Caronia's approach to science fiction, and his concept of the cyborg, needs to be situated in the field of his grassroots political experiences within the Italian movements between the sixties and seventies, and beyond. For Caronia, science fiction was a tool with which to analyze society, culture and politics, and

2006), which provides the reader with essential tools to understand the main concepts described by Dick in his novels. We thank Domenico Gallo for his involvement in the first phase of editorial mediation with the ShaKe publishing house for the English translation of this book.

highlight the contradictions and power structures embedded within them.

The concept of the cyborg is not to be understood literally, and is not solely related to technology and the machine: it is a complex organism that embodies the signs of our present, by becoming an interface between the past and the future; it is the coexistence of the possible and the impossible, epitomizing the passage from modernity to post-Fordist society, while representing the end of utopian beliefs, and the inspiration for people to keep on believing.

### The Politics of the Hybrids

At the end of the seventies, a very crucial moment in the history of Italian grassroots and radical Left movements, Antonio Caronia—who had just abandoned Trotskyism and his political engagement in the Fourth International—became involved with the collective *Un'ambigua utopia* (An Ambiguous Utopia), co-publishing the homonymous magazine between 1977 and 1982. As Antonio Caronia and Giuliano Spagnul point out in the introduction to the recently published anthology of the original issues, he started his political experience in the collective, attracted by the attempt "to read science fiction from the left,"[4] to create an understanding of fiction, popular culture and entertainment, by including them in a critical political discourse. At the roots of this intellectual and political engagement is the idea of "estrangement," referring to the process of making familiar what is alien, and vice versa. This perspective is linked to the concept of *defamiliarization*, which was developed by Viktor Shklovsky in his essay "Art as Technique" (1917), and used extensively by the avant-gardes, in an attempt to dismantle culture's hierarchies and holistic truths, by making art objects unfamiliar while

4    Antonio Caronia and Giuliano Spagnul, eds., *Un'Ambigua utopia: Fantascienza, ribellione e radicalità negli anni '70*, vol. 2, no. 6–9 (Milan: Mimesis Edizioni, 2009).

experienced. In rendering the unfamiliar comprehensible, by playing with unusual juxtapositions, unexpected combinations, and deconstructions of reality, science fiction becomes a methodology of cultural criticism, while generating an understanding of power structures embedded in our everyday life. In dealing critically with aliens, cyborgs and artificial organisms, Antonio Caronia meant to interpret our society as a collage of incongruities, without necessarily solving them, but leaving them open for reflections on possible political and tactical practices derived from encounters with the "alien."

As Antonio Caronia points out, the idea of politicizing science fiction is related to the practice of transforming scornfully excluded issues and arguments into politics, working upon the fractures between public and private, and between the pleasure of reading literature and being actively engaged in society. At a time when the movement of 1977 was criticizing many of the extreme Left's traditional political practices, the emergence of new needs and aspirations (as Caronia remembers, many people were inspired by the writings of Agnes Heller and the feminist approach of those years) caused the consolidated political militancy all kinds of problems; the strategic use of science fiction became a way to explore more experimental practices, generating constructive semantic confusion, *ambiguous utopias,* in which the use of the body was central. Science fiction in this sense becomes "a contribution to the understanding of who we are, to the development of other forms of sociability, of other codes of communication, of some new modest local theory. Aware that these paths are rough and inevitably ambiguous."[5]

5    Antonio Caronia, "Un'Ambigua Utopia" [An Ambiguous Utopia], in *MIR, Men In Red,* magazine edited by the Collective of Radical Ufology, no. 2 (1999). This is a quote from a text entitled "Incarnazioni dell'immaginario" originally published in the book *Nei labirinti della fantascienza. Guida critica a cura del collettivo "Un'Ambigua Utopia"* (Milan: Feltrinelli, 1979), 15, my translation from Italian into English.

12 These paths were not only followed on a theoretical level; they also gave space and importance to the role of the body and interpersonal communication, trying to connect intellectual engagement with elaborations of new forms of expression. At the end of the seventies this attitude was put into practice by the Italian collectives close to the *Indiani metropolitani* (Metropolitan Indians), the so-called creative wing of the movement, which developed within the underground movement and the emerging scene of *social centers*, inspired by representatives of the U.S. Beat Generation and its writers and poets like Jack Kerouac and Allen Ginsberg, the French Situationists and the Dadaist movement. Many members were extremely critical of the prevalent strict Marxist doctrines, and strived to dismantle dialectic power structures by creating ludic interventions, often based on the destructuration of language and communication, and by using disguise, playfulness and provocation as tactics.

In 1978, Antonio Caronia and the Ambiguous Utopia collective (along with Franco "Bifo" Berardi and Freak Antoni) took part in Alfabeta Group's "La produzione mentale" (Mental Production), performing an unorthodox speech using the imaginary slang of Vega 4. That same year, the collective organized a conference entitled Marx/z/iana (Marx/t/ian), where it tried to stage performative practices using costumes and masks, stressing the limits of the traditional academic format. This art of camouflage not only showed a playful methodology of intervention, but was embedded in the belief that the strange and the extravagant can express hidden conflicts in politics and society, making the body the main vehicle of a critique of production processes, bringing such contradictions into the experience of everyday life. Common people are therefore at the center of investigation, and very often the people that are "dispossessed", "aliens" and precarious are the ones who embody signs of power, becoming the *simulacra* of the contemporary.

Therefore, when Antonio Caronia writes about the cyborg, he is writing about all of us: the cyborg becomes a subject of political reflection on the development of contemporary society, where technology, and its strict relation with the body, assumes a crucial role. We are all cybernetic organisms, in the sense that we all experience hybrid conditions of being, our blood and flesh intertwining with economic growth and technological development.

### The Future of the Im/Possible

The dismantling of science fiction realized by the Ambiguous Utopia collective aimed to transfer the literary genre into the interstices of society and through the concrete practices of everyday life, beyond the adventures described in the novels. As Caronia points out, the idea was to work on the "cognitive potential" of science fiction, to better understand society and to act more efficiently within it.[6] Therefore, the objective was also to dismantle the concept of utopia itself, and the belief in technological progress, which had characterized much sci-fi literature until the sixties, as described in the first part of *The Cyborg*. Since the seventies, the development of science fiction has been related to the development of post-industrial society and the information economy, reaching a dystopian point of narration in which progress is no longer celebrated.[7] The celebration of the progressive expansion of human potential through machines reaches a point of involution with the emergence of a global crisis of production, in the transition from industrial to post-industrial capitalism. Since the end of the seventies, many experimental writers already envisioned such a transformation (i.e. Philip K. Dick, James G. Ballard, and

6 Antonio Caronia and Giuliano Spagnul, "Storia di una cassetta degli attrezzi," in *Un'Ambigua utopia: Fantascienza, ribellione e radicalità negli anni '70*, ed. Antonio Caronia and Giuliano Spagnul, vol. 1, no. 1–5 (Milan: Mimesis Edizioni, 2009), 7.

7 As Caronia points out, this interpretation was not only suggested by the *Ambiguous Utopia* collective, but also in *Robota Nervoso* magazine and in the book *Fantascienza e comunismo* [Science Fiction and Communism] (Milan: La Salamandra, 1979) by Diego Gabutti, and internationally, in Haraway's essay "A Cyborg Manifesto."

William Burroughs), and during the eighties the science fiction genre came to document the crisis, as Caronia suggests, taking shape within cyberpunk literature. Caronia states that science fiction dies when "society is no longer capable of planning its own future,"[8] and when new imaginaries emerge from the contamination of bodies and technologies. The advent of the cyborg brings with it the death of science fiction, and according to Caronia, the cyberpunk movement represents science fiction's swan song.[9]

The fact that cyberpunk is defined as an underground movement requires a dedicated reflection, and it is very specific to the Italian grassroots context of the eighties and nineties. In 1990, the Decoder collective, which gave life to ShaKe Edizioni (ShaKe Editions) in Milan, published the book *Cyberpunk, Antologia di testi politici* (Cyberpunk, Anthology of Political Essays), edited by Raf "Valvola" Scelsi. This book became central to the development of a political vision of cyberpunk literature in Italy, a phenomenon that needs to be specifically situated among Italian radical movements, the scene of squatted social centers and the history of Italian hacker culture and underground digital networks.[10] As we read in the introduction to the *Cyberpunk Anthology*, "cyberpunk is read essentially as a political phenomenon, such as techno-urban writing, mirroring the changes produced on the

8    Caronia, Antonio. 2009. "La FS è morta, viva la FS!," in:
     Hamelin, Futuro Presente, no. 22. www.academia.edu/298069/
     La_fantascienza_e_morta_viva_la_fs_.
9    Ibid.
10   Antonio Caronia wrote extensively on the Italian cyberpunk phenomenon in
     his books, which are at the moment only available in Italian. To get deeper
     into the development of Italian cyberpunk as a political movement, read
     the chapter "Towards the Cyber Utopias" (58–90), and in particular the paragraph "Cyberpunk in Italy" (68–75) in my book *Networking, The Net as Artwork*
     (Aarhus University: DARC Press, 2008). This issue is later analyzed by Marco
     Deseriis in the chapter "Italienischer Cyberpunk," in *Vergessene Zukunft.
     Radikale Netzkulturen in Europa*, ed. Clemens Apprich and Felix Stalder
     (Bielefeld: Transcript, 2012), 137–143.

new social subjects by the contemporary".[11] The last paragraph of the introduction describes the core of the editorial (and political) approach adopted by the Decoder collective:

> Today Cyberpunk offers the opportunity to all cultural operators and to the movement to open a huge new field of production of collective imagination, capable of disrupting the existing imaginative blockade, that has long oppressed us. The inspiring themes of Cyberpunk […] belong through history, future evocations, and fascinations to the countercultural movements. We must reappropriate them collectively.[12]

In chapter 7 of this book, Antonio Caronia describes the connections between international cyberpunk literature and the development of a new social imaginary based on the interconnection between man and machine, particularly through the works of William Gibson, Bruce Sterling and John Shirley, and David Cronenberg films like *Videodrome* (1982) and *eXistenZ* (1998). Just like the Decoder collective, Caronia also "appropriates" cyberpunk literature in this context to describe a deep transformation of society, the same as that described by Bruce Sterling in the introduction to the *Mirrorshades Anthology* (1986), which Caronia considers to be the "Manifesto" of cyberpunk literature. Here technology's contamination of the body, and the cyborg's emergence, mirroring the development of the information society, appear evident. For Caronia, this means using the cyborg to question authority and to mix different layers, immaterial and material, in the critical and political understanding of our being active subjects in post-industrial society.

11    Raf "Valvola" Scelsi, "Mela al cianuro", the introduction to the book *Cyberpunk. Antologia di testi politici* [Anthology of Political Essays], ed. Raf "Valvola" Scelsi (Milan: ShaKe Edizioni Underground, 1990). My translation from the Italian.

12    Ibid., 33.

16      The second part of this book, "The Post-Fordist Cyborg", was added by Caronia in 2001: here we find his reflections on the contemporary cyborg, when the metaphor of the alien moves from the concept of being external to our body (well exemplified by early science fiction) to inhabiting the nerves beneath our skin, merging with our post-industrial everyday life. Drawing upon the theoretical works of Michel Foucault, the cyborg, a mix between the material and immaterial, the natural and the artificial, becomes the simulacrum of a bio-political body, inscribed with information technology and new means of production, power mechanisms and flows of pleasure.[13] The techno-imaginary becomes a tool for analyzing production flows, raising many questions related to our becoming, and the dismantling of the holistic self, as Donna Haraway suggested, by viewing the cyborg as a fluid element in constant transition.

In the last two chapters of *The Cyborg*, dated 2001 and 2008 respectively (the latter was added by the author to the last edition of the book), Antonio Caronia reflects on the most recent development of the cyborg imaginary. In the chapter "Cyborg Ecstasy" Caronia points out that, in the last decades of the twentieth century, openness to the "possible" became increasingly more connected to the critical appropriation of technology than to the means of production, thus questioning the traditional leftist political approach developed by Marxism after the mid-twenties. Technology introduces new possibilities embraced by avant-gardes, such as the development of experimental visual languages, and political and social critical engagement. This affirmation should not be interpreted as a techno-utopian determinism, contradicting Caronia's oft-stated critique of technological progress, but rather as a way to imagine

13      See Antonio Caronia's teaching documents, *Michel Foucault: per una genealogia del soggetto*. M-Node research seminar series given by Antonio Caronia and Amos Bianchi, NABA, AA, 2011–2012. Audio recordings at: http://archive.org/details/MichelFoucault_PerUnaGenealogiaDelSoggetto.

political empowerment through the conscious use of technology. 
This aspect is very much present in the development of the
Italian digital underground movement, in hacker culture and the
reflection on artistic practices as forms of critical understanding
of everyday life. Antonio Caronia was a perceptive researcher
from the outset of the emergence of digital culture in Italy, often
involved in many collective initiatives organized by social centers,
universities and local artistic and independent political contexts.
He was also very active in promoting emerging experimental
artistic initiatives based on the creation of multiple identities or
multiple-use names, from Luther Blissett (1994) and Darko Maver
(1998), to Janez Janša and his previous project *Problemarket* (2001),
and Anna Adamolo (2008).[14]

As described above, the first reflections on virtual reality and
digital technologies in Italy were put into practice by many
activists, artists and hackers in the social center scene and
DIY circuits between the eighties and the noughties, giving life
to many independent collectives, groups and artistic projects
nationwide. Technology was seen as a central element in the

14   See the essays collected in, Antonio Caronia, *Universi Quasi Paralleli. Dalla
     fantascienza alla guerriglia mediatica* (Rome, Cut-Up Editions, 2009). See also
     Antonio Caronia, "From Multiple Names to Wu Ming," a four page feature
     from *Pulp Libri* #29 [an Italian bi-monthly review of books] (January-February
     2001), available at: http://www.wumingfoundation.com/english/giap/
     Giapdigest4.htm; Caronia Antonio, "Darko Maver Doesn't Exist. Prank of Art,
     Art of Prank," published in *l'Unità*, 14 February 2000, online at: http://www.
     nettime.org/Lists-Archives/nettime-l-0003/msg00076.html; to know more
     about the Problemarket project, see: http://www.aksioma.org/problem-
     arket; for a reconstruction of the Anna Adamolo project, see: Tatiana
     Bazzichelli, Loretta Borrelli, and Antonio Caronia, "Anna Adamolo: Practical
     Critique of Ideology," *Digimag* 41 (February 2009), online at: http://www.
     digicult.it/digimag/issue-041/anna-adamolo-practical-critique-of-ideology,
     and the chapter "The Anna Adamolo Multiple singularity" in my book *Net-
     worked Disruption. Rethinking Oppositions in Art, Hacktivism and the Business
     of Social Networking* (Aarhus University, DARC Press, 2013), 124–135 (available
     in pdf format: http://disruptiv.biz/networked-disruption-the-book). The
     complete collection of essays written by Antonio Caronia is available at:
     http://naba.academia.edu/antoniocaronia.

process of liberation, from the use of Bulletin Board Systems (BBSes) and independent servers and networks, to free software and hacker projects. It becomes a tool of appropriation of information capitalism, a means to bend its limits and expose its bugs. It is among these circuits that we should situate the reflections of Antonio Caronia—in the analysis of the collective power of networks, and the constructive potential of the *general intellect*. But at the same time, the *obscure potential* of technology to reproduce mechanisms of alienation and power structures is still present, once again adopting a double level of interpretation that is never absolutist or one-sided. The question of belief in the *possible*, and at the same time its destructuring, is still present in the last chapter, "From the Cyborg to the Posthuman," where the metaphor of the posthuman is seen as a tool to once again criticize a deterministic and mono-dimensional conception of human nature. According to this point of view, openness to the possible is specifically embedded in the acceptation of its relativeness, which can only be understood by assuming the plural and fluid perspective of the hybrid—the cyborg.

# THE CYBORG

## ANTONIO CARONIA

*To Maria*
*to close the circle*

# Preface

If the life of a book were comparable to that of a human being
(an unutterable anthropomorphic temptation that, despite being
aware of its inconsistency, we always succumb to), this book
would have reached the age of majority some time ago. In fact, it
made its first appearance in 1985 with the Theoria edition, which
was then reprinted in 1991. Out of print for a while, it was repub-
lished in 2001 with the ShaKe edition, its original text partially
rewritten and modified, and a totally new second part added.
For this third edition (for the same publisher) the text was again
rewritten but, bar the corrections of material errors and small
adjustments, it is the same as the 2001 edition, with the addition
of a postscript that updates the discourse linking it to the Italian
and the international debates on the so-called "posthuman."

The author cannot deny a certain degree of satisfaction in
seeing that this little book conceived twenty-four years ago has
in some ways resisted the march of time, growing and showing
itself capable, if not of providing answers, of at least helping
and orienting the questions of readers interested in understanding some of the more controversial and central phenomena
of today, like the hybridism of human beings and technology,
tackling the relationship between human biology and culture in
the imaginary and real life. It is said that once a book is written
it leaves the tutelage of its author and becomes, not only a
"citizen of the world," but also the property of its readers, who
use it and interpret it in ways the author might not even have
dreamed of. But some books (perhaps many) often return to their
author, and inspire him to reread, rethink, update and, at times,
contradict them. If this should happen, as it did with the book
you are now holding, it is not because it was ahead of its time,
as some excessively kind readers have pointed out, but more
simply because its subject matter, the man/machine hybrid, has
gone from being a purely fantastic figure to being an everyday
experience in little more than thirty years. Back in the fifties

 and sixties, our relationship with machines had already become more routine, but it was a relationship between different and still clearly recognizable partners. However, since the eighties, technology, as Bruce Sterling rightly puts it, has begun to get under our skin. We witnessed the growth of a number of customs that saw technological gadgets go from being mere fellow travelers to becoming an extension of ourselves. A large part of this process, as observed by Derrick de Kerckhove, was stressed by going from analogical electricity (extension of our physical body) to digital electricity (extension of content and mental processes). The cyborg, that for a good part of the nineteen hundreds was a limited analogy of our relationship with machines and technology, literally took shape towards the end of that same century. The phenomenon is perhaps more general: according to Arthur C. Clarke, any sufficiently developed technology is indistinguishable from magic, thus every metaphor in the post-Fordist world appears destined to become literal. And the first stage of this literalness, much like in Kafka's story, is our body. This is why the figure of the cyborg could lead to the posthuman.

This term, as I will try to show through the course of this book, has been a source of countless misunderstandings. However, the posthuman debate at least has the merit of having brought the question of relations between continuity and discontinuity in the development of humans to the fore. To what processes does a term like "posthuman" allude? Today, has proximity, frequentation and hybridity with technology reached such a stage that *Homo sapiens* may now claim to have overcome his dependence on biology? Does the posthuman era also mean a post-biological era? Put in these terms, it is clear that the questions may only be met with a negative answer. As observed by many, starting with Denis Diderot back in the eighteenth century, the contrast between "natural" and "artificial" is not compatible with the characterization of the species, considering that man's technical and manipulative activities, on a par with his linguistic and symbolic ones, are no more than the developments of our basic biological legacy, and of our brain in particular. After all is said and done, culture is our biology and Robert Marchesini rightfully reminds us that for some years now the trend in hybridity is not simply a characteristic of twentieth and twenty-first century humanity: what is happening today apropos of our relations with physical and virtual machines has always taken place throughout the process of hominization, in the field of relations with other animal species. In the final analysis, it depends on our marked leanings towards caring for the young. In this sense, the extremist and post-speciesist interpretation that the various "trans-humanist" movements give of the posthuman prospect is unfounded and possibly even risky.

But once the fundamental continuity of *Homo sapiens'* technical approach has been established, it is very difficult not to see an increase in quality, a radical lack of continuity in the process of reproduction and production of life on this planet. Therefore the cyborg—if we don't just mean in the original and limited description of a "natural" body to which mechanical, electrical or chemical components are added, but in the broader sense of a being whose "original" biology is modified by any process that is finalized and controlled externally (for example, through genetic modification)—presents itself as characteristic of a phase in which the organism's spontaneous functions no longer act as a natural barrier to the interventions of hybridity and of modification. These no longer occur "downstream" of the basic biological devices (as in the case of traditional animal and vegetable biotechnologies, with their means of selection and hybridism, and the creation of new species and varieties not exis-tent in nature), but "upstream" of those devices: man can now modify them (more or less) immediately and permanently, and "in real time" somehow, giving rise to an unprecedented control over and restraint of biological processes. Does this mean that the posthuman will allow us to leave the *Homo sapiens* environment, that biotechnologies will configure the birth of a new species (*Homo technologicus* or *simbionte*, names proposed by Giuseppe

 O. Longo) no longer regulated by biological evolution, but by the combination of biological and cultural evolutions? If this question makes sense, then the answer to it is firstly that *Homo sapiens* has always been *Homo technologicus*, that the direction of the "technicalization" process of human life has not changed in the last forty years with respect to 100,000, 500,000 or a million years ago, and that what we are witnessing is no more than an extraordinary acceleration and extension of that same process; and thus there is no hurry to announce the birth of a "new species." If there is something we can call "human nature," it is nothing more than an extraordinary behavioral predisposition to plasticity, flexibility and to diversity, as shown by the vast variety of languages and cultures created by human beings since they first appeared on this planet: we are beings of possibility, in perennial and dogged combat against necessity. The new phase of hybridism with technology does not represent a deviation from the premises, does not have us exit the birthplace of the species. But at the same time we cannot deny that the unusual extent of man's intervention in the planet's biological (and geological) evolution will not raise questions concerning the long-term consequences of our cultural conduct. This is indeed an absolute novelty: human beings have never shown the potential to modify "natural" processes in such a broad, widespread and profound way. But this is not enough for a univocal and determined response to the question that we posed ourselves. Quite simply, despite the hybridization and convergence of the two spheres, the spatial and temporal scale of the biological processes clearly remains more ample and penetrating, and incomparably more widespread than the scale of cultural processes: and thus at this stage of the process we are not capable of guessing all the possible consequences of the latter, and perhaps neither the direction.

And so we come to the problem of judging the values, of questioning ourselves on the desirability or less of such a process. In this field, as in many others—but here perhaps more acutely— the view of the sociologist or contemporary historian cannot be

neutral, however inflexible the intention is of coming up with the 
most complete and accurate picture of what happens, putting
in parenthesis every judgment on the goodness, legitimacy and
desirability of these processes. This is not possible because
inevitably the same choice of the conceptual instruments of
analysis, of pertinent criteria, of subject matter, refer to inevitable
preconceptions, to basic directions that condition, whether we
like it or not, even the most aseptic description of a process.
Donna Haraway reminds us that all knowledge is situated: there
is never any talk from a neutral and abstract place, but rather
from a historically determined position, filled with expectations,
prospects and desires. I hope this book's standpoint is clear
right from the start. However, I consider it helpful and honest to
open with at least a basic methodological orientation. Without
understanding this, it will instead be easy to accuse the book's
discourses of technological determinism, or of being an apology
for the status quo. The author does not ignore, and says so
explicitly on more than one occasion, that today hybridization
with technology is one of the privileged ways through which very
a great and compulsory process of subjection of human life to
the dispositive of global economy is realized. Today's cyborg is
post-Fordist, in the sense that its merging with technology, its
love of technology, and the increase and intensification of the
relational and cognitive opportunities that digital technologies
allow—all of which add up to being the instrument through which
a fragmented labor force, physically divided and dissipated but
connected and brought into discussion at a virtual level—is
forced into a gigantic process of capitalistic growth that sees no
difference between work and leisure, between the office and the
playground, and between times for public life and private life.
Whether we like it or not, we all work twenty-four hours a day for
the global economy that takes full advantage of the possibilities
offered by technology to keep us in an unstable, precarious,
underpaid and subordinate position. This is the contemporary
form of slavery. This new intellectual and cognitive proletariat—
the hacker class, as termed by McKenzie Wark—has every interest

 in overturning the logic of this process, in using the relationship
with machines to set it free, and not to confirm its inferiority.

Now, all this unleashes a series of problems relative to social
dynamics, to a rethinking of the imaginary, to the opening of
channels of experience and experimentation, of proposals and
the spread of conflicts. It is not this book's job to elaborate on
the subject. But what I believe we should exclude is the illusion
that the best way to oppose this state of things is to entrench
ourselves in nostalgia for the past and to demand the return
to situations that have already passed us by. This is instead a
temptation often indulged in by a section of radical thought,
especially some wishing to represent the continuity, albeit with
the necessary updates, of Marxist tradition. But didn't Marx
teach us that the circumstances of upheaval and continuous
innovation created by capitalism were the most advantageous
for the revolutionary process? Didn't he encourage us to take
advantage of every opportunity that the "development of the
productive forces" offers regarding the theoretical and practical
criticism of productive relations? (I deliberately use a classical
dictionary that is probably in need of updating, if only to highlight how distant today's imitators are from their maestro). The
theoretical backwardness and practical impotence of the Left and
Center Left political parties and trades unions in Europe vis-à-vis
the gigantic reconstruction of global capitalism and the breaking
up and weakening of the working classes is there for all to see.
But it won't be the very weak demand for a return to the classic
welfare state that will resist the devastating effects brought
on by the process of the labor market becoming precarious. It
won't be a call for a "return to politics" that will put an end to the
dictatorship of the post-Fordist economy over the life of men and
women of the world. And it won't be the nostalgia for a fading
"humanism" that will exorcize the advance of a posthuman condition that instead begs to be lived, analyzed and understood all
the way in order to be criticized, not in its inescapable aspects,

but for the tragic and frightening consequences caused by the conduct of those with both economic and political powers.

# PART ONE

# THE DAWN OF THE MODERN HYBRID

# Introduction

The twentieth century was unusually rich in extraordinary and monstrous figures, as were the centuries bridging the Medieval and Modern Ages. Some of those forms returned, while other completely new ones were created in the great science fiction stories on paper and the silver screen. The attitude towards these beings might no longer be the same as it was during the Medieval Ages, but it still incarnates a sense of fear that, not totally free of concerns over ecological catastrophes and nuclear holocausts, is a more than plausible hypothesis. Palingenetic dreams resurface, and "rebellions against the modern world" with the scornful confidence of those who love to inhabit ruins (and who in some cases also love to create them). But that history is a circle, destined to return to the point of departure, is just a rough and bad interpretation of the "eternal return" hypothesis. These fears and anxieties, just like anything else that justifies a certain similarity between the Late Modern Age and Late Middle Ages, according to an analogy that has circulated for quite some time in western culture and of which Umberto Eco's *The Name of the Rose* was the most illustrious example, are the legitimate offspring of our status, of the change of era that we are living: a transformation of the basics and the ways of an associated life so radical that it has been called an "anthropological mutation" more than once. Naturally, this mutation is not provoked by a technology considered to be an autonomous agent: from different but converging points of view, this is the belief of admirers of all things wonderful and the overly harsh critics of the computer revolution. Technology is the child of human activity, and as such is not the cause, but the obvious symptom, intermediary element and symbol of the transformation that enfolds us. This does not detract from the fact that when the change is magmatic, overpowering and pervasive, man struggles to recognize his own impact on what is happening around him, preferring to attribute the reasons for the mess surrounding him to autonomous figures who ominously rise up against him. This is why our era is populated with monsters, as was the autumn of the medieval era that saw in molecular construction a change as intense and devastating as the one we are living today.

However, being situated at the crossroads of two not completely separate, but relatively autonomous traditions, the contemporary monster is genetically more complex than its medieval counterpart. Naturally, like its predecessor from the classic and medieval world, it is a "wonder," something to be seen, to be made known (the root of the Latin *monstrum*, "monster," is the same as the Latin words *monstrare*, "to show," and, apparently, *monstrare*, "to caution, to counsel" as well as "to warn against," but also "to exhort, to chastise"). In the classical world, as in the medieval world, the monster is a *natural* creature, whose existence occasionally serves to demonstrate nature's unlimited flair for change, to restore it to a primordial state of indifference between man and his environment, to mean (as in Saint Augustine) a complex and incomprehensible order willed by the creator, with its embedded aesthetic valence. However, being *natural*, this monster plays on a few constitutive parameters: be it man or animal—and the dividing line is never that clear-cut—it is either the result of the restriction or the hypertrophy of certain organs, of certain sections of natural bodies, or (as is mostly frequently and strikingly the case) it is a hybrid, an unknown contamination of the most familiar bodies in nature. This characteristic of the classical and medieval hybrid guarantees it will be an object of "scientific" inquiry in the period of transition between the Medieval Ages and today, as in the repertories of Ulisse Aldrovandi and Ambroise Paré. But in the fifteenth and sixteenth centuries the figure of the hybrid had already transferred part of its physiognomy to a newer character, one born out of traditions of thought and the "marginal" cultures of medieval Europe, and from certain alchemic and Talmudic currents: *the artificial man.*

*Homunculus* or *golem*, the artificial man of the Renaissance, testifies to the proud project of repeating the divine creation, and the creature's inevitable rebellion against the creator. But

it also introduces itself as the first, elusive nucleus of reflection 
in the process of "nature's artificialization" that accompanies
industrial society's entire development and the revision of the
collective imaginary to which it is connected. Combined with
the extraordinary and magical precision of a new craftsman-
ship that cut its teeth in the new art of watch-making and the
manufacture of mechanical looms for the textile industry, the
idea of the artificial man materialized in the haughty and serene
eighteenth-century automatons of the likes of Vaucanson and
Jacquet-Droz. For a couple of centuries the simplification of
Newtonianism entrusted the "machine" concept with a contra-
dictory anthropological paradigmatic role, thinking itself capable
of taking that decisive and resolute step forward in the study of
man. In little more than a century, from Mary Shelley to Karel
Čapek, the artificial creature's inevitable rebellion was consolidated in literature. In the thirties, science fiction inherited
the "creature" and popularized it, first in comics and then on the
silver screen. A race of new monsters was finally amongst us, and
it was time for the next invasion.

If the *Frankenstein* monster and the *R.U.R.* robots caused
amazement and anxiety in their "overly human" feelings, and
aspirations in the artificial bodies of double creatures, but
were nonetheless distinct in respect to man, today's even more
enigmatic problem is understanding and classifying a creature
whose human body and machine body are irreversibly entwined.
Cyborg, a tough but expressive name, is the anacronym of
*cybernetic organism.* "A fictional or hypothetical human being,"
as defined in the seventies in Webster's Dictionary, "modified
in order to adapt to life in non-terrestrial environments via the
substitution of artificial organs and other parts of the body." It is
a somewhat simplified definition, touching on only a part of the
cyborgs that Brian Stableford (in Clute and Nicholls' *Encyclopedia
of Science Fiction*) classified as "adaptive cyborgs" and "functional
cyborgs." The third category, "medical cyborgs,", is not only
the most widespread in literary and film science fiction (as in

**36** the seventies TV series *The Six Million Dollar Man* and *The Bionic Woman*), it also includes human beings who have gone beyond the "hypothetical" condition to live amongst us, not only in flesh and blood, but in flesh, bone, metal, plastic and power circuits, with their pacemakers made of artificial veins and arteries (and now hearts too). In any case, together with whatever problems relate to the precise definition of this new being, the hybrid is back. However, just like its classic and medieval ancestor, the disparate, inaccessible elements that constitute it are no longer taken from the alphabet of forms that nature puts at the disposal of our imagination. This time the hybrid appears even more sacrilegious, because it complicates (folds together) in a single being the creator and his creature, the body par excellence, that which by the very nature of the body should be more distant. Man and machine fused into a single organism. Is this the triumph or the definitive defeat of the radical materialism of the "man-machine?"

# 1

# Cosmographies

The cyborg figure appears quite early on in American science fiction, in the twenties, and is more or less a contemporary of the robot and the android that science fiction had taken from far older traditions and contexts. In those years, the term still had not been coined (that would be not until 1960, and not by a writer of science fiction, but by two doctors of the Rockland State Hospital in New York, Manfred Clynes and Nathan Kline, while finalizing their work on astronautics), but there can be no doubts as to the nature of the new beings. The man of 8,000 BC, with a clockwork mechanism in his head, with which he travels through time and unknown dimensions (*The Clockwork Man*, by Edwin V. Odle, 1923); the immortal brains wrapped in metallic casings that plan to bounce Earth from its orbit to theirs in order to conquer it (*The Comet Doom*, by Edmond Hamilton, 1928); Professor Jameson, who survives the destruction of the human race thanks to the encasing of his brain, and then wanders the worlds of the twenty-fifth century (*The Jameson Satellite*, by Neil R. Jones, 1931, the first in a long and successful series): these are the first man-machine hybrids of science fiction pulp.

**38**   As one can see, the origins of the cyborg are connected to travel through both space and time. In the above books, the cyborg is the element of a clearly immeasurable and perhaps even menacing cosmography, but in some way still orderly. As in medieval times, the monster still inhabits "another world". However, that which in medieval cosmology was the other hemisphere, the kingdom of Satan, the desert, or every other place distant and unknown, has now journeyed into sidereal space in an extreme attempt to save the order of the cosmos by extending its frontiers. There is more: this first alien cyborg repeats the close relationship between places and monsters typical of the relationships between travel and medieval bestiary, and synthetically expressed by Roger Bacon, "The place in which they are born is the principle that presides over the generation of things." At the time, travelers did not marvel at encountering monsters (often mere evidence of their presence) in the places they passed through. The link between places and monsters was both of the aesthetic and moral type, and rested on the metaphorical consideration that Earth was a living body: the base parts of the earthly body corresponded to vile and degraded beings. A comparable relationship seems to link the comet to its inhabitants in Hamilton's novel which, because of its simplicity, can be considered indicative of this early narrative on cyborgs. The hybrids of *The Comet Doom* populate the solid nucleus of a comet, far from the tail's poisonous gases. They were once "normal" beings, their science superior to that of humans: cybernetics came later, to compensate for the shortage of food in their world. Another shortage (this time of radioactive materials necessary to run their machines) triggers the evil plan to capture Earth (that was rich in them): annulling the sun's gravitational pull at the moment in which the comet passes closest to our planet thus launching Earth into space to penetrate the comet, whose gases would completely wipe out humanity and supply the aliens with space and boundless energy. The correlation between the evil of these beings (motivated by environmental needs) and the noxiousness of their habitat is quite evident: there is no need after all to expound on the characteristics of this deadly omen that the comet has shared with us since antiquity. At least in its intentions, this cyborg is alien and opposed to man. "They weren't men, they weren't of human form", the author declares peremptorily, only to contradict himself on the next page when talking of a nervous system, brain and blood circulation; after all, incongruences of this type abound in the "heroic" science fiction stories of those years: it is true that it will be possible for a man, a traitor, to undergo the same operations as the aliens, becoming one of them in every way, without the slightest difficulty. The strangeness is highlighted by the exquisitely "robotic" look of the artificial body (towards the end of the sixties, we will find illustrations of robots that would appear to take on this type of appearance to the letter):

> Imagine a man with a body of shiny, black metal instead of flesh: a large metal cylinder that, in place of legs, has four metallic limbs much like those of a spider, and in place of arms four metallic tentacles, like those of an octopus. This was the being: it wasn't much taller than the average man. Instead of a head on its cylindrical body there was a cube, a metal box that could turn in any direction. There was a disc of soft white light on each of the cube's four faces.[1]

> Whether evil aliens or clockwork men of the future, merciless conquerors or good-natured, cybernetic professors wandering amongst the stars, these "sidereal" cyborgs no longer share the same vision of the world nor the cognitive strategies of the medieval monster. The latter, in the moment in which it broke the natural "order" of things, revealed it in negative; the moment in which it presented itself before man as an indecipherable enigma, it provided an answer at the same time, at least Saint Augustine's answer on the mysteriousness of God's designs, "in knowing where and when to create what is or what was necessary".

---

1    Edmond Hamilton, *The Comet Doom* (1928).

Our cyborgs, at least for the moment, do not appear to prompt such radical questions, nor make a relevant contribution to a new design for the universe, except for the obvious fact that it has grown beyond measure. While the cosmic spaces are the new austral hemisphere, it will be relatively "reasonable" to find new generations of monopods, mandrakes and cannibals, this time in the form of aliens resembling octopuses, spiders and insects (the famous BEM, bug-eyed-monsters). The cyborgs of the twenties are nothing other than a more "technologized" variation of these aliens.

But things soon begin to get complicated. The spread of the eighteenth-century mechanistic version of Newtonian physics was the final blow to the symbolic valences with which the universe's geometry in medieval vision was equipped, in which high and low, the known and unknown corresponded, as we have seen, to "moral" qualities and thus postulated a well-defined type of inhabitant. In the mechanistic vision, space is a container (to the more naïve) or a mental function (to the more hardened, who take the lesson of Kant into account), but homologous and isotropic nonetheless: it no longer has direction or privileged dimensions. In principle, the monster would thus be free to live wherever it likes, making nonsense of the Baconian axiom. And space, even if unknown, is in its essence wholly predictable and open to travel. This is where it becomes complicated. The theoretic practicability, even if only fantastic for the moment, of this new homogenous and undifferentiated space reveals to modern sensibilities an aspect that in previous epochs was totally inconceivable. Because it is potentially accessible from any direction and at any distance, space regains a frightening dimension due its immensity. And science fiction makes a very diligent appraisal of this. Once again, the crucial point is the journey and its exploration; the modality is a merging of imagination and science, not new in western culture.

The theory of relativity, put forward in the early years of the twentieth century, quickly became the dominant paradigm in the scientific community, accepted also by writers of science fiction. In this sector, in the second half of the thirties, a new orientation began to assert itself, more preoccupied with the "plausibility" of the fictional construction (also from a point of view of scientific coherence) than the *space-opera* of the previous decade. The theory of relativity, without questioning the space model inherited from classic physics, but by simply refining it and making it more complex, nevertheless introduces a limit that turns out to be of particular importance. Its equations in fact imply that no body can be animated by a speed faster than light (equivalent to roughly 300,000 kilometers per second). So how can one imagine interstellar travel lasting hundreds, thousands, millions of light years? Amongst the various solutions thought up by science-fiction writers, one quickly stands out "thanks to its great abstraction and formal elegance":[2] "hyperspace" was first articulated in science fiction in *The Mightiest Machine* (1934) by John W. Campbell, who was editor of the *Astounding Science Fiction* magazine and the principal exponent of the new science fiction trend. The hypothesis of hyperspace travel had already been explored in several English "scientific tales" of the previous century (*Flatland* by Edwin A: Abbot; *A Plane World* by Charles H. Hinton; Giovannoli also found traces of the same in the works of H.G. Wells): our three-dimensional space is immersed in a "vaster" space with a major number of dimensions (at least four), exactly like the two-dimensional surfaces that we know make up part of three-dimensional space.

Just as two distance points on a surface (a sheet of paper, for example) can be brought into contact simply by folding the space between them, one can imagine doing the same with two distance points in space, by "folding" the three-dimensional space that contains them. A spaceship may pass instantaneously from one point to another by applying a hypothetical curving

2    Renato Giovannoli, *La Scienza della Fantascienza* [The Science of Science Fiction] (Milan: Bompiani, 1991), 175 [trans. Robert Booth].

technique, a three-dimensional space torsion within the pluri-dimensional space, or hyperspace, that contains it.

Born from a need to render interstellar travel less "fantastic", soon enough hyperspace  became the focus of many of the fears associated with its immensity. Too inaccessible to be a daily experience, the leap into hyperspace is a leap into the unknown with all its dangers and fears. The collective imaginary takes its revenge on "scientific" plausibility. Any man exposed to space travel will be changed by the experience: the simple sight of new constellations silhouetted against the backdrop of black space, crude light no longer refined by the atmosphere's refraction, and the frightening contact with a deep space monstrously distorted by being plunged into new dimensions generate demoniac and seductive visions, new illusory realities in which man's body takes on totally unknown forms and functions. If for the characters of *Star Wars* the leap into hyperspace is a naturally fantastic experience, but innocuous nevertheless, one cannot forget the phantasmagorical and scary geometry that suddenly appears before David Bowman in his voyage beyond Jupiter at the end of *2001: A Space Odyssey*, until his more radical mutation.

> There, in some corner of eternal space, an atrocious death awaited, death and horror that man had never encountered before embarking upon interstellar travel [...]: the impact of a psychic, ferocious and devastating blow dealt the living occupants of the spaceship.[3]

This is how the mysterious entities awaiting the intergalactic travelers in a 1955 story titled *The Game of Rat and Dragon* by Cordwainer Smith were described: beings who the telepathists on board the spaceship "liken to the dragons of popular terrestrial antique traditions, beasts more astute than the beasts, devils more tangible than the devils, maelstroms hungry for life and hate made up of unknown means from tenuous and subtle

---

3    Cordwainer Smith, *The Game of Rat and Dragon* (1955).

materials from interstellar space." Once again, the monster has its own space, an environment well suited to it. But the monster's turf no longer defines, as it did in tales of medieval travel, an ordered cosmography; no longer constitutes, to put it in Franco Cardini's words, the "confirmation of the creation's divine order."[4] If all of space is the same, neutral and homogenous, the monster will be able to flourish anywhere: it is the cosmography of a new chaos, a map of confused and uninterpretable signs, a jumble of soothing follies under the tenuous and calm veneer of predictability, ready to leap out and attack the minds of men.

Also because absent in the reports of these future voyages, so extraordinary and so full of today, is a certainty that was present in medieval travel: the presence of man as a fixed point, an element of comparison, a unit of measurement (even in his misfortunes and limitations) posited by God to distinguish between normal and abnormal, order and disorder. Man constantly risks being excluded from interstellar travel. Nothing like the vastness of space reveals his weakness and fragility (caused by the disappearance of God's hand that until now had supported him in his more hazardous endeavors). In the reports of voyages to the new southern hemispheres, "space-sickness" is one of the more frequent complaints: intolerable acceleration, solitude, visions and hallucinations, the impossibility to communicate. Imponderability and discomfort caused by the marked lack of room for the first and now familiar astronauts of the Apollo and Soyuz spacecraft are no more than the first intolerable steps of this mysterious but already operative syndrome. In reality as in fantasy, the relationship with the machine (the computer and its extraordinary ability to calculate and control processes) is the obligatory route that man must take to explore space. The man-machine hybrid, the cyborg, is thus a natural candidate for this new endeavor. Monstrosity, alienness, insinuates itself into

4    Franco Cardini, introduction to Clauce Kappler, *Demoni Mostri e Meraviglie alla Fine del Medievo* [Demons, Monsters and Wonders at the End of the Medieval Age] (Florence: Sansoni, 1983), 8 [trans. Robert Booth].

that same being that, with its testimony and its presence, should guarantee the voyage objectivity and purpose. Chaos is no longer restricted to man's exterior, but to his interior as well. The *race of devils,* of whose coming Frankenstein feared, established itself permanently in his house. If until the thirties the cyborg was still basically an alien, almost exclusively of the "brain-in-a-metal-box" type, hostile to man and hell-bent on invading Earth (as in the above mentioned stories, or in the 1932 *The Time Conqueror* by Lloyd Arthur Eshbach; the only exception being the Zoromes who "cyborged" Professor Jameson in the series by Neil R. Jones), it now begins more frequently to be a mutated man, in many cases to render him more adapted to space exploration.

This type of cyborg is somehow codified in the fifties by Cordwainer Smith (a writer of whom little is said today, despite the considerable influence he had on numerous writers throughout the ensuing decades), both in its "weak" form, as a man who has basically maintained his nature while developing a particular relationship with the machine (*The Burning of The Brain,* 1958; *Golden The Ship Was – Oh! Oh! Oh!,* 1959, then resumed by Samuel R. Delaney in *Nova,* 1968; *The Lady Who Sailed The Soul,* 1960), and in its "strong" form, as a being so mutated it has completely or partially lost all trace of humanity (*Scanners Live In Vain,* 1950). It is in this second version that the "spatial" cyborg returns in a series of short stories and novels by Thomas N. Scortia (*Sea Change,* 1956), Anne McCaffrey (*The Ship Who Sang,* 1961), Arthur C. Clarke (*A Meeting With Medusa,* 1971), Frederik Pohl (*Man Plus,* 1976), and Barrington J. Bayley (*The Garments of Caean,* 1976).

# 2

# Morphologies

The first and most simple cyborg is also the most radical: a brain in a metal box. Nothing survived of the man's body (or of the alien's) except his most "noble" organ that guarantees its cerebral functions. Everything else is a replica, nearly always grotesque, as has been seen, of the human form or its variant, that of the anthropomorphic robot. The most famous and most evil of these "boxed" brains is the one described by Curt Siodmak in *Donovan's Brain* (1943), which was also made into a film.

Even Catherine L. Moore, who in 1944 wrote a powerfully innovative story on the cyborg (*No Woman Born*) in which she did away with the stereotype of evil and for the first time tried to think of the new hybrid's psychology, resorted to the brain-in-the-box model: this time the box is not a square built and ungainly robotic body, but a highly refined reconstruction of a female body (the brain belongs to Deirdre, a famous singer and dancer who, only in this way, could be saved from a fire). There is no doubt that the image of the brain closed in an artificial container exercises a strange and perverse fascination on writers, and not only those of science fiction, seeing that Jorge Luis Borges and Adolfo Bioy Casares gave us their parodic form of the cyborg in *Cronícas de Bustos Domecq*. Cordwainer Smith introduces a bizarre variant of the brain-in-the-box, the laminated brain, a kind of animal cyborg, in which the brain (of a mouse, for example) is not connected to any machine, but serves to contain the entire personality of a human being that may then be used as a source of strange holographic projections. The laminated brain appears as a "a black plastic cube with shimmering silver contact-points gleaming on its sides," and was obtained by "stiffening the brain with celluprime and then veneering it down with at least seven thousand layers of plastic of at least two molecular thickness."[5]

Naturally, though not depicted as aprioristically evil, the artificial body cannot fail to arouse a sense of irritating anxiety, despite the unnatural perfection conferred upon it by the artisan. The anxiety is far greater knowing that a human brain lives and works behind the metal. The amazed and bewildering description of the new Deirdre in *No Woman Born* expresses admiration, but also a sense of uneasiness.

> She had only a smooth, delicately modelled ovoid for her head, with a sort of crescent-shaped mask across the frontal area where her eyes would have been if she had needed eyes. A narrow, curved quarter-moon, with the horns turned upward. It was filled in with something translucent, like cloudy crystal, and tinted the aquamarine of the eyes Deirdre used to have. [...] She turned it a little, gracefully upon her neck of metal, and he saw that the artist who shaped it had given her the most delicate suggestion of cheekbones, narrowing in the blankness below the mask to the hint of a human face. [...] As for her body, he could not see its shape. A garment hid her. But they had made no incongruous attempt to give her back the clothing that once had made her famous. [...] The designer had solved his paradox by

5    Cordwainer Smith, *Think Blue, Count Two* (1963).

giving her a robe of very fine metal mesh. It hung from the 
gentle slope of her shoulders in straight, pliant folds like a
longer Grecian chlamys, flexible, yet with weight enough of
its own not to cling too revealingly to whatever metal shape
lay beneath. The arms they had given her were left bare, and
the feet and ankles. And Maltzer had performed his greatest
miracle in the limbs of the new Deirdre. It was a mechanical
miracle basically, but the eye appreciated first that he had
also showed supreme artistry and understanding. Her arms
were pale shining gold, tapered smoothly, without modelling,
and flexible their whole length in diminishing metal bracelets
fitting one inside the other clear down to the slim, round
wrists. The hands were more nearly human than any other
feature about her, though they, too, were fitted together in
delicate, small sections that slid upon one another with the
flexibility almost of flesh. [...] She looked, indeed, very much
like a creature in armor, with her delicately plated limbs and
her featureless head like a helmet with a visor of glass, and
her robe of chainmail.[6]

This is obviously a contest between the artisan and his model,
resolved with sufficient skill by the former. Beings of this type,
however, can only be made of unique parts, and the challenges
they bring are just as unique, idiosyncratic. The moment they are
"mass produced", the boxed brain will inevitably resemble the
robot (this was the observation made by Asimov in comparison
with Neal R. Jones' Zoromes). The "functional" cyborg, the one
conceived for space exploration, as well as its "repeatability,"
requires a sort of cheapness: only the indispensable parts of the
human body are substituted or modified. The new form derived
from it is no less intriguing. We see an example of this in *The*

---

6    Catherine L. Moore, *No Woman Born* (1944). In the most extraordinary way,
     Deirdre's description recalls the fantastic beings in painter Giovanni Battista
     Bracelli's etchings (*Bizarie di varie figure*, 1624; see Paolo Portoghesi, *Infanzia
     delle machine* [Rome-Bari: Laterza, 1981], 10–11).

 *Garments of Caean*, an adventurous-philosophical novel by Englishman Barrington J. Bayley:

> She focused the screen on one specimen to examine it
> closely. Like its brethren, it had been extensively modified
> by deep surgery and the incorporation of artificial organs.
> Embedded in its skull was a turret-like device which she
> guessed was connected directly to the brain. The eyes were
> hidden by the black goggles which seemed to be riveted into
> the eye-sockets. The nose had been removed. [...] The chest
> had been replaced entirely by a metal box-like structure.
> Likewise the abdominal wall was substituted by a flexible
> corrugated shield, making it resemble the abdomen of some
> type of grub. [...] The genitals had been left intact and floated
> flaccid and loose. The mixing of man and machine continued.
> From limbs, backs and sides projected an assortment if
> devices and turrets. [...] The modified men were far from
> being identical to one another. The machine-organs they
> incorporated varied from individual to individual, as though
> a division of function existed between them.[7]

Bayley's cyborgs inhabit interstellar space, living there without
any form of protection, and are thus in need of particularly
radical modifications. At other times, the demands are quite
different: living inside the spaceships, for example those
described by Cordwainer and driven by the pressure of light, with
enormous sails that extend for tens of thousands of kilometers.
In these spaceships (prior to the discovery of hyperspace, that
which this author called "planoforming") voyages last dozens
of years, which requires a considerable reduction in the pilots'
biological rhythms, allowing them to stay alive the entire
duration of the transport. The effect is obtained through a series
of surgical interventions on the pilot's body, such as inserting
valves in the arteries, artificial colostomies to regulate the bodily

---

7    Barrington J. Bayley, *The Garments of Caean* (1976; published in the U.S. in
     1978).

fluids with the insertion of catheters, needles connected to the 49
brain to reduce physiological activities in the desired way (*The Lady Who Sailed The Soul*). The forefathers, so to speak, of the functional cyborgs can be found in another Cordwainer Smith story, *Scanners Live In Vain*, and are indeed the scanners. Here we are still at the start of the space era. Man has been to the *Up-and-out*, to outer space, but discovered that here nestled the "first effect", "the great space sickness", that induces in man a desperate need for death until he does actually die. To travel into space, man must therefore be transformed: all his sensory organs responsible for pain are disconnected from the brain, his internal organs (like the heart and lungs) no longer able to send signals to the rest of the body. This "disconnected" man is supplied with a series of control tapes with which to regulate his vital signs by hand. He is permanently marked by the "radiating scars around the instruments, the stigmas of men who had gone to the up-and-out". Smith indicates two categories of cyborg like these: the ordinary ones, called *habermans*, criminals or undesirables, who are sentenced to hard labor in space, forced to undergo surgery, and have no direct control over their own tapes; whereas the scanners (controllers and observers) voluntarily choose mutilation in order to work as pilots or officers on the spaceships. Formally honored by the community and the government, but in reality barely tolerated for their looks and habits (having no control over their muscles, they walk heavily, have "thunderous and deafening" voices, and their faces become "horrendous misshapen masks"), the scanners have formed an exclusive corporation and harbor a secret hate for the other men. However, they may temporarily regain full control of their senses and enjoy a quasi normal life by subjecting themselves to brief periods of "cranching", the use of a device that temporarily restores normal neural connectivity: hearing, smell, taste, muscle and voice control. Here is how they themselves describe their condition in a sort of catechism that makes up part of the rituals of their corporation, and that recalls the similar litanies of the men-beasts in *The Island of Doctor Moreau* by Wells:

"And how, O Scanners, are the habermans made?"

"They are made with the cuts. The brain is cut from the heart, from the lungs. The brain is cut from the ears, the nose. The brain is cut from the mouth, the belly. The brain is cut from desire and pain. The brain is cut from the world. Save for the eyes. Save for the control of the living flesh."

"And how, O Scanners, is flesh controlled?"

"By the boxes set in the flesh, the controls set in the chest, the signs made to rule the living body, the signs by which the body lives."[8]

Cordwainer Smith doesn't give very precise information on the techniques of the construction of his scanners. And it is perhaps this vagueness that renders them all the more fascinating. However, twenty-six years later, in *Man Plus*, Frederik Pohl would expand quite faithfully on the space cyborg studies of Clynes, Kline, Del Duca and other NASA scientists to paint a more "realistic" picture:

The eyes were glowing, red-faceted globes. His nostrils flared in flesh folds, like the snout of a star-nosed mole. His skin was artificial; its color was normal heavy sun tan, but its texture was that of a rhinoceros's hide. Nothing that could be seen about him was of the appearance he had been born with. Eyes, ears, lungs, nose, mouth, circulatory system, perceptual centers, heart, skin—all had been replaced or augmented. The changes that were visible were only the iceberg's tip. What had been done inside him was far more complex and far more important. He had been rebuilt for the single purpose of fitting him to stay alive, without external artificial aids, on the surface of the planet Mars [...]. Pulse, temperature and skin resistance sensor pads clung to his shoulders and head. Probes reached under the tough

8    Cordwainer Smith, *Scanners Live in Vain* (1950).

artificial skin to measure his internal flows and resistance. **51**
Transmitter antennae fanned out like a peasant's broom
from his backpack. Everything that was going on in his
system was being continually measured, encoded and trans-
mitted to the 100-meter-per-second broad-band recording
tapes.[9]

And in the following chapters Pohl does not miss the opportunity to furnish us with further details of the cyborg's new
sensory systems, its daily life, its new metabolism. Such an acute
preoccupation with verisimilitude, albeit futuristic, such a precise
insistence on the "point to point" correspondence between the
natural body and the artificial body, return the hybrid to a realist
narrative atmosphere, albeit within the science fiction genre, in
accordance with Pohl's choices of the seventies. The emphasis,
beyond the adventurous plot, is placed on the character's interior
conflicts and the dramatic dimensions of his condition. But when
the cyborg is introduced to illustrate a contentious, sarcastic or
simply ironic debate on the hyper-technological trends of our
world and their inauspicious consequences, the figure of the
brain-in-the-box or one of its variants is once again the most
exploited. This is what happens in David R. Bunch's bitter and
violent (and often boring and monotonous) *Moderan* (1971), a
world described as completely artificial and covered in plastic,
and ruled by "displaced" men. In a rare moment of self-irony, one
of them describes himself:

> [A]t my ease I do not look like a god. I must look more like
> a suit of old armor once would have looked if it had in the
> ancient days rolled in some thick-sliced bacon and then gone
> to bed on a bridge truss. Yes, we look like walking steel shells
> with flesh piping, in Moderan, and we think of wars and good
> pounding. To live forever, to be our true bad selves—those
> are our twin destinations.[10]


9    Frederik Pohl, *Man Plus* (1976).
10   David R. Bunch, *Moderan* (1971).

52	And even when Borges and Casares' alter ego, Bustos Domecq, has to satirize the longing for immortality (*Los Immortales, 1967*), he encounters nothing but disturbing cubes:

> The narrow space was round, white, low-ceilinged, with neon lighting and no window to combat the claustrophobia. It was inhabited by four characters or furniture. They were the same color as the walls; the material, wood; the form, cubic. Each cube had a smaller one on top of it, with a short grate above an aperture that looked something like a letter box. Taking a closer look at the grate, one was amazed to see a pair of eyes following one's every move. At intervals, the apertures let loose with a chorus of sighs or indistinct little voices whose words were quite unintelligible. Their positioning was such that each cube found itself face to face with another, while flanked by another two to create a reunion of friends.[11]

Borges and Casares, insisting on the geometric and material form of their immortals, on the paralyzing and claustrophobic atmosphere that surrounds them, create a cyborg figure that is at the antipodes of the one imagined by Clarke in *2001* and developed (for too many pages) in the sequel *2010: Odyssey Two*, which describes an immaterial being wandering through space, transported by perverse, highly mobile and electromagnetic waves. "The brain," says gerontologist Narbondo, who suggests Bustos Domecq turn himself into the new being definitively, "irrigated day and night by a system of magnetic currents, is the last animal stronghold in which gears and cells still coexist. The rest is Formica, steel, plastic. Breathing, eating, procreation, movement, and even excretion are all obsolete stages. The immortal," he concludes, "is a property".[12]

11	Jorge L. Borges and Adolfo B. Casares, *"Los Immortales,"* in *Cronícas de Bustos Domecq* (1967) [trans. Robert Booth].

12	Ibid.

# 3

# Bodies and Mechanisms

The cyborg is the final frontier (for now) of man's confrontation
with machines, one that has been present in Western culture
for at least three hundred years, its roots going back even further. The antithesis between man and machine comes from that
between "natural" and "artificial", but does not identify with it
entirely. In fact, machines are not only creations of man, they
already exist in nature. In the modern age, the first to formulate this observation and so draw on the possible consequences
was René Descartes: in his mechanistic vision of the world,
everything can be explained based on material and its movement
in space. The universe is a gigantic machine, animals no more
than robots. Contrasting this is man, the hub of a conscious
activity that cannot be explained in corporeal and material terms,
and therefore presupposes the existence of another principle,
not furnished with enhancement but with thought (*Principia
Philosophiæ*, 1644). Descartes, however, admitted that the human
body's entire function is explainable in purely mechanical terms:
therefore even man's body is a machine, likewise an animal's
body. The establishment of this similarity between body and

 machine (that other thinkers, like Hobbes or La Mettrie, will radicalize by denying the existence of a "deliberating substance" and by reinstating the notion of material movement) is in reality typical of modern science, and refers to a mutation of the "body" in the transition between antique and medieval societies, still influenced by the remnants of "magical" thought and modern society.

We can find this analogy a century before Descartes, in Andreas Vesalius's anatomic charts (*De humani corporis fabrica*, 1537–1543) that ushered in new medicine by releasing its foundations from the confines of classical texts, as was the custom, and initiating a new practice in empirical observations, penetrating the body through the dissection of cadavers. To liken the human body to a machine is the analogy from which one may imagine the body being made up of organs, observable and learnable, of which one may describe the functions and base a scientific discussion on the ensuing descriptions. The Age of Reason will develop this point of view rigorously and relentlessly: the automatons of Vaucanson, Jacques Droz, and Maillardet, with their extraordinary gears and precision mechanics that mimic certain movements of the human body in such a refined way, depend on this conception in the final analysis. These creations are registered within a line of thought defined with great clarity by Diderot: man, in his every activity, is a product of nature, and therefore in the final analysis his every creation is "natural", even when he proudly conceives it as an innovation (*Pensées sur l'interprétation de la nature*, 1753). One may never surpass nature, no matter the sophisticated and daring heights man's ingenious work might reach, there is no significant distinction between natural and artificial. Naturalism and mechanism work well together in the illuminist seventeenth century, at least in France. Anthropology is a specialized branch of cosmology, and the machine may cause amazement or per-plexity, but certainly not anxiety. The homologation between the body of man and the body of the machine temporarily concludes the process started two centuries earlier with Vesalius: a process that aimed at maintaining a unitary picture of the world, even after the dissolution of classical and medieval cosmology and anthropology.

In the medieval vision, just as in that of classical antiquity, the body still conserved traces of its role as the fundamental social mediator that it had held in so-called primitive societies. In these, the most significant elements of collective life (birth, initiation, marriage, sickness, death) were accompanied by a strong social investment in the singular body, of which contemporary western societies retained little more than a blurred memory. Consumed within those events were processes of adaptation to the changes in the social codes concerning the collective, a veritable "creation of meaning", since the latter was never, as for us, given once for all, but was meant to be defined time and again in relation to the continuous homeostatic adjustments of the balance between man and nature. Levi-Strauss,[13] analyzing societies that don't write, described this process as an excess of significance, a "plethora of meaning" in so-called "pathological" thought, versus a reality lacking in significance. This, something that José Gil called "fluctuating signifier", must be temporarily pinned down during the course of events that indicate the resolution of a crisis, and it is precisely this fixation that, with the creation of a new sense and new correspondences between man and the cosmos, signals resuming control of the situation. In general, the shaman is responsible for regaining control by identifying a material object as the support of the fluctuating signifier whose free and uncontrolled character threatened social equilibrium. If sometimes, for example during the potlatch, the support came in the shape of objects or artefacts exchanged or donated, more often than not it is found in the human body.

In these societies, on getting better, the body of a sick person, for example, always reveals a piece of extraneous matter or

---

13    Claude Lévi-Strauss, *Structural Anthropology* (New York: Basic Books, 1963), 181.

even a part of himself which incarnates, rather than the "cause" of the sickness, the proof of the sickness and its eventual cure: a practice that has survived on the fringes of contemporary society to this day. In a culture of this type the body comes across as a network of signs, not always transparent but effective nonetheless, sometimes as an indifferent support to the symbolic processes, taken from the usual processes of significance and open to being bombarded by all sorts of languages. Scarcely involved in the processes that psychology would call identification or the construction of "self," here it is directly implicated in the holy dimension, and together guarantees a primitive and immediate unity between man and nature. This is why, in the shamanic experience, the human corporeal form can easily transform into that of an animal.

Establishing the body as an object of scientific investigation, which we have conventionally gleaned from Vesalius's new anatomy, is possible only by overcoming the magical solidarity that the body enjoys with its environment, and the "natural history" it helped to write. Sixteenth and seventeenth-century materialism, in its naturalistic meaning, looks very much like an attempt to recreate, on neither magical nor holy grounds, the solidarity between body and nature, bravely incorporating every human activity. So on one side, with La Mettrie, d'Holbach and, to a lesser degree, Diderot, we take a look at the material of a sentient character, while on the other we take a general look at scientific discoveries and technological inventions like playing "catch-up," a way to become increasingly more compatible with nature. The problem, no different to that of the shaman in so-called primitive societies, is about channeling the energy that circulates freely, not allowing it to cause any damage and, if possible, making it produce positive and beneficial results instead. It is clear that science and technology share the vision that will dominate a large part of the nineteenth and twentieth centuries, of a linear, undefined and ever burgeoning growth of man's productive forces in all their forms, including machinery.

Machines that therefore can only oppose man in conjunctures  because they are his creation. As far as man's body is concerned, it will revert to being a network of gestures, but only because its functions (both physical and mental) reflect a universal mechanical order that treats mental activity as a particular case in a still unfamiliar way, a situation destined to change sooner or later.

Nevertheless, the progress and development of the new productive forces, in essence the new machines built and marketed in this first phase of the Industrial Revolution, did not convince everyone. As early as the eighteenth century, the first criticisms came from an area of Europe not yet at the center of technical and economic innovation, Germany, and were relatively isolated. In the years in which they were published, the stories by Ernst Theodor Amadeus Hoffmann seemed little more than the bizarre outpourings of a contorted mind. However, the robots, the extraordinary machines that amazed and delighted the courts and salons of Europe, turned into grotesque apparitions, bearers of ruin and death. Within years, the evil robot will become one of romantic Germany's most popular characters, will also cross the English Channel to become the indeterminate and monstrous artificial creature of Mary Shelley's *Frankenstein*, and will go on to become one of the mainstays of the fantasy genre, inaugurating a tradition still with us today. In Karel Čapek's *R.U.R.*, when the automaton changes into a robot it will continually rebel against its creator and determine his ruin. One will have to wait until Isaac Asimov's *I, Robot* in 1950 to have an artificial creature capable of living peacefully and beneficially with mankind, despite having a problem or two of its own. What happened? The man's body, separated from the system of symbols that lent coherence to society and to a primitive world, taken from the immediate and elastic rapport of his fellow creatures and with the other elements of nature that gave it a sense of stability, established himself in that new modernity called "self," the system in which the events of a "psychic life" had never been described before because they were unknown (and, because it is the mind that describes itself, presumably non-existent). That human psychic activity is based on corporeal fundamentals is an old materialistic hypothesis, unsustainable in its "naïve" and radical eighteenth-century form, but reformulated in a disapproving way by psychoanalysis:

> A person's own body, and above all its surface, is a place from which both external and internal perceptions may spring. It is seen like any other object, but to the touch it yields two kinds of sensations, one of which may be equivalent to an internal perception. Psycho-physiology has fully discussed the manner in which a person's own body attains its special position among other objects in the world of perception [...]. The ego is first and foremost a bodily ego; it is not merely a surface entity, but is itself the projection of a surface. The ego is ultimately derived from bodily sensations, chiefly from those springing from the surface of the body. It may thus be regarded as a mental projection of the surface of the body [...].[14]

The importance of the perception of one's own body in psychic life has become an inalienable fact, and kindles such a general consensus that one may find this concept in the most unexpected places. Staying with science fiction, here is how for example it is formulated in List's *Cultural Compendium*, the fictitious anthropological text invented by Bayley, the date of its writing unknown but which can presumably be placed hundreds of years in the future:

> Every creature having a complex nervous system makes use of body images. The body image is an image of itself: the knowledge that the creature has of its physical existence, a knowledge that sets itself halfway between conscious and unconscious perceptions. Much has been said about whether or not the body image has a genetic base, or if

14    Sigmund Freud, *The Ego and the Id* (1923).

instead it is the result of conditioning. In order to solve the 
problem, experiments were carried out on human vol-
unteers subjected to total amnesia, and attempts made to
have them accept alternating images of animals or robots
as their own. The results were convincing. [...] Some of the
subjects admitted to having "dreamed" of being what they
saw as their own bodies: a dog, a bear and, in one case, even
a butterfly.[15]

Undoubtedly, the experimenters that List (and Bayley) talks about
knew of Zhuang-Tzu's analogous dream, of a couple of millennia
earlier...[16]

What is certain is that, at a given moment, the machine's
increasing capacity to simulate and emulate human behavior has
combined with the changes taking place in the status of the body,
and has given rise to the creation of a differently featured and
named "artificial man," who has assumed the functions of man's
"double" collective, evil and ruinous, in which, as in other doubles
of fables and literature, a return of the reject is embodied. To the
double "human" of fantasy literature, the "artificial" double of
science fiction (meant in the broad sense, to include *Frankenstein*
and *R.U.R.*) one can add an ambiguous character, one halfway
between machine and man. The reject, in a manner of speaking
"social", who in this way returns, has a more direct approach to
the workings and position of the machine in collective life: like
all rejects it has something very familiar, so familiar it ends up
being put aside. It is the presence, real and metaphorical, of the

15    Bayley, *The Garments of Caean.*

16    "Once Chuang Chou dreamt he was a butterfly, a butterfly flitting and
      fluttering around, happy with himself and doing as he pleased. He didn't
      know he was Chuang Chou. Suddenly he woke up and there he was, solid
      and unmistakable Chuang Chou. But he didn't know if he was Chuang Chou
      who had dreamt he was a butterfly, or a butterfly dreaming he was Chuang
      Chou. Between Chuang Chou and a butterfly there must be *some* distinction!
      This is called the Transformation of Things." Chuang Tzu, "Discussion on
      Making All Things Equal," in *The Complete Works of Chuang Tzu*, trans. Burton
      Watson (New York: Columbia University Press), 49.

machine in our daily life, at all levels, its increasing essentiality to man's life, as decisive as it is remote and invisible. But doesn't literature perhaps have, amongst other things, the power to reveal what is hidden, to render the invisible visible?

Whereas the material and concrete eighteenth-century automaton built by great machinists had a reassuring effect with regard to man's physical excellence (so complex it deserved to be copied) and to his mind (so acute it was capable of imitation), the robot, the android and the cyborg of modern-day science fiction instead signal the decline of man as we know him, or think we know him from what history and routine have passed on to us, and the birth of a new man, similar in appearance to the creature that he himself built, but in some ways already autonomous. They do it by asking a question, though not new, but unquestionably actual ("what is man?"), in the most emotionally and narratively effective form of "how does one distinguish a 'natural' man from an artificial one?" Though an explicit response is rarely given, an implicit response is often contained in the modification of the question, even in its radical reversal: "how can an artificial being become an authentic man?" Science fiction, from Cordwainer Smith to Asimov, to Simak, is filled with stories of civil rights battles won by robots, androids and *underpeople*. Giovannoli talks of a continuous "becoming": from machine to man via the robot and android stages, and from man to machine via the cyborg stage.[17] During the course of this "becoming" described by science fiction, the cyborg represents a hypothetical radical response, the birth of a new species: a response, naturally, that is not definitive, and in no way settles the problems; on the contrary, it presents innumerable others.

In her new metal body, the reconstructed Deirdre of *No Woman Born* poses problems for Maltzer, her maker, who is afflicted with an ambiguous syndrome, halfway between Pygmalion and Frankenstein. On one hand, Maltzer is rightfully proud

17    Giovannoli, *La Scienza della Fantascienza*, 24 [Trans. Robert Booth].

of the machine that he has created, "of such inhumanly fine proportions" that it replicates the old body of the woman, but with totally new vocal and motor possibilities. On the other hand, however, he is convinced that Deirdre is no longer human: "She hasn't any sex. She isn't female any more," and has also lost three of the five senses, the oldest and most deep rooted in man's corporeal system: touch, taste and smell. "Sight is a cold, intellectual thing compared with the other senses. But it's all she has to draw on now. She isn't a human being any more, and I think what humanity is left in her will drain out little by little and never be replaced." But Deirdre was once an actress and a singer, a female entertainer, and wishes to return to the stage. Maltzer wants to spare her any stress and disappointment, convinced as he is that she will not be accepted by the audience.

Like her maker, Deirdre is also convinced of her irreparable and radical uniqueness, "[a] sort of mutation halfway between flesh and metal. Something accidental and... and unnatural, turning off on a wrong course of evolution that never reaches a dead end."[18] She has no doubts about her loneliness, present and future. But the tenacity with which she experiments with all the new possibilities of her body, the stubbornness with which she decides to prepare her new show, reveal a strong trace of humanity still within her; and the stage is the means to manifestly highlight her links with the original species. Naturally, Maltzer is wrong: Deirdre's show is a huge success, and the new figure's sensual element overwhelming, as though the cyborg wanted to get revenge for the maker's mortifying observation regarding her femininity (it's worth remembering that the author, Catherine L. Moore, is a woman).

*No Woman Born* is the first science fiction story in which the cyborg sheds the clothes of an alien originating from some distant star to take on the look of a more familiar alien (if the paradox is allowed), namely man. Man intended as human being,

18    Moore, *No Woman Born.*

naturally, because Deirdre, as we have seen, is a woman, and she opens the door to other female aliens, characters in seventies science fiction, some of whom, significantly, will still be cyborgs (Helva in the already-mentioned *The Ship Who Sang*, and Philadelphia Burke in *The Girl Who Was Plugged In*, published in 1973 by James Tiptree whose real name, in spite of the masculine pseudonym, is Alice Sheldon). Catherine L. Moore's story highlights the problem of cyborg identity, and consequently that of man too. As a technological hybrid, the cyborg cannot help but carry an enigma both internally and externally, just like its distant predecessor, the mythical sphinx. Algis Budrys individualized this radical query of identity in his novel *Who?* published in 1958. American scientist Lucas Martino, the victim of an accident in a West Berlin laboratory, is abducted by the Soviets and returned a few months later with an artificial head and arm: the extraordinary operation, they say, was necessary to save his life, otherwise he would have died due to the injuries he sustained in the accident. But the Americans can't be sure that the person restored to them in that condition is really Martino, and suspect he might be a spy sent by the Russians to steal data on the highly important and top-secret project that he worked on before the accident. The secret service is mobilized to gather proof that will decide the cyborg's true identity. They will never find that proof. The man with the metal head will retire to an isolated country house, far from prying eyes, even though the reader (having had his doubts, like the secret service, during the course of the book) now knows that he really is Lucas Martino. The novel (very much like Jack Gold's 1974 film of the same title) paints a picture of extreme gloom in the lonely life of the new being, whose egg-shaped head (much like Deirdre's) prompts disgust and repulsion from all the humans who come into contact with him. By now, in most of the literature on the cyborg, this situation is paradigmatic: the hybrid is seen by man to be a sort of new freak, and at first glance the horror that it provokes is stronger than curiosity. In fact, Budrys has Martino, who has just arrived in New York, run the tragic gauntlet of urban estrangement that takes him to a squalid hostel in Bleecker Street. Here, the concierge shows no distaste on seeing the metal face: "The clerk was used to seeing cripples. The rooms upstairs were full of one kind or another."[19] Martino's body, like with all cyborgs, and particularly in space, performs deeds far superior to its normal human counterpart, but is considered by others to be that of a "cripple." Cordwainer Smith accentuated this aspect: his scanners are deprived of senses, and when they want to go back, albeit temporarily, to being complete men, they must first undergo *cranching*—as cyborgs, their deafening voices and grotesque faces render them unacceptable to man. One of them has even learned to speak softly and to artificially control its face muscles in order to cultivate more normal social relationships. Beings of this type cannot help but swing back and forth between a spasmodic wish to be reintegrated into humanity and a proud desire to remain within the corporation (that is when the cyborg isn't an exceptional and unique individual, like Deirdre or Martino). Sometimes the rhetoric of space conquest and progress serve as a consolation. Bart, one of the *cyborgized* space pilots described in *Sea Change*, while trying to convince some human interlocutors, talks of himself and others like him in the third person:

> They aren't men anymore. They might not even be humans anymore. But they aren't machines [...]. They have something that normal men will never have. They have found a role in the grandest dream man has ever dared dream. And it takes guts... a lot of guts to be what they are. Not men, and yet part of the greatest thing that man has ever looked for.[20]

And the story ends with the vision of "a metal confraternity crossing outer space: tense brains enveloped in a metal skin, in a single organism reaching... reaching for the stars."

19    Algis Budrys, *Who?* (1958).
20    Thomas N. Scortia, *Sea Change* (1956).

Fortunately, we are rarely forced to swallow a cocktail of broken-winded rhetoric of this type. At other times, the hybrid's propensity to return to its primitive form helps it be explicit in the face of the first, immediate reaction. When Smith's *scanners* find out that space sickness has been eliminated, that space travel will be accessible to normal human beings, they feel that their profession is threatened and so decide to kill the inventor. The historical and narrative rationality embodies itself in the *scanner* Martel, who quite by chance witnesses the *cranch* meeting when, looking in from the outside, he becomes aware of all the horror of their condition; he therefore decides to warn the inventor and allow all the *scanners* to return to their human form. However, this type of happy ending is not common. More often than not, the cyborg form is presented as a definitive state, and the horrific effect it has on us is attributed to our quality as men of the present—this will no longer exist in the future. However, even in this case, some of the narrative choices made by authors betray an uneasiness with the hybrid; for example, by hiding the man's original body inside the machine. In Bayley's novel, *The Garments of Caean*, the space travelers come across another species of cyborg other than the one described in the previous chapter: giant spacesuits, about three and a half meters tall, minus their legs, minus a visor, that, driven by an autonomous propulsion system, wander about in an asteroid zone, emitting radio signals. On capturing one, the human explorers, to free the human it presumably contains, have no choice but to cut open the suit. No sooner done, they find a naked human form with atrophied arms and legs, completely linked to the suit by a tangle of cables, tubes and catheters. The suit, to all intents and purposes, is its body, with sensory, locomotive and phonatory organs, and the being never leaves it: this species has also developed a form of artificial sex fully capable of reproductive activities, in the shape of a tooth that protrudes from the "male" suit to penetrate the sheath of its "female" counterpart. The expedition's sociologist comments:

It means that his own body-image of himself doesn't include **65**
anything we would recognize as a human being. When he
thinks of himself as a person, the picture in his mind is that
of his suit's exterior. Probably he isn't even conscious of his
biological body, except as a sort of internal organ or essential
core. As far as he is concerned, the suit *is* his body.[21]

Even the "shell-brains," the "minds" that steer the spaceships in
*The Ship Who Sang*, are miniaturized bodies within titanium suits,
hidden for security reasons within the ship's central column. They
are the bodies of babies born with irreparable malformations
but with a normal brain, who, after just a few months of life, are
trained to live in their new metal bodies, after which they receive
schooling to suit their future occupation:

> Shell-people resembled mature dwarfs in size whatever their
> natal deformities were, but the well-oriented brain would
> not have changed places with the most perfect body in the
> universe.[22]

From their column, the encapsulated minds see and hear
everything that occurs on the ship, communicate with the "arm,"
the human partner who drives the ship with them, and who they
choose themselves, and with whom they can even fall in love,
which is what will happen to Helva, the story's leading character.
This equilibrium between the values of corporeal beauty,
intelligence and sensorial power established by McCaffrey (the
original deformity is the price the cyborg "pays" for its new skills)
has a slight consolatory flavor to it. Tiptree, who resumes the
theme, flips the situation around instead, dramatizing it to the
hilt. Delphi, the beautiful holovision star in *The Girl Who Was
Plugged In*, is a "waldo," a remotely controlled cybernetic system,
or rather an automaton, "eighty-nine pounds of tender girl flesh
and blood with a few metallic components,"[23] controlled at a


21    Bayley, *The Garments of Caean.*
22    Anne McCaffrey, *The Ship Who Sang* (1961).
23    James Tiptree, *The Girl Who Was Plugged In* (1973).

distance by a human operator in a shell with the brain linked to the communications system that animates the machine. For the female operator, Philadelphia Burke, an ugly and unhappy girl, Delphi's life epitomizes a thrilling experience she would be unable to live if it weren't for the automaton that gives her life. Apparently divided into two components, human and machine, the figure of the cyborg reunites in death, when Delphi's young lover, having discovered her nature as a mechanical doll, kills her together with Burke. Just like Helva in *The Ship Who Sang*, Burke also manages to escape an unhappy destiny thanks to her integration with the machine; like the latter, the former also experiences the trauma of separation (her human partner dies during the voyage, while Helva, well protected by the metal, is saved), but the happy ending that follows in McCaffrey's story, with a predictable speech on the "sense of duty" and the "continuity of life", is a far cry from the dramatic conclusion of Tiptree's story. Here the integration of man and machine is pushed to such a degree that stopping the latter means killing the former. Just like television's cyborg *The Six Million Dollar Man*, in which the naked eye cannot tell which parts of the body are human and which are artificial.

The enigma that the cyborg carries inscribed in its body is therefore the same one recalled by the androids in Asimov's "detective" series (*The Caves of Steel* and *The Naked Sun*), and the replicants in *Blade Runner* that Ridley Scott adapted from the novel by Philip K. Dick *(Do Androids Dream of Electric Sheep?)*: what is this being I find in front of me, man or machine? Is it a product of nature, or of human ingenuity? If the question, as far as the android is concerned, is epistemological (that is to say, concerning the possibility of having certain knowledge of the two beings, man and android, whose origin is surely different), as far as the cyborg is concerned it is ontological. Wondering if a cyborg is man or machine is like doubting our beliefs and our convictions on what is man, his nature or, from a linguistic point of view, his definition. And if in the dualistic tradition of Western thought the line of demarcation between human and nonhuman is more on the side of the mind than the body (Descartes had identified the distinctive characteristic of man with respect to animals), it cannot be denied that in one's conscience the corporeal form is closely associated with mental activity. But, as we have seen, by identifying man's body as the object of a specific discipline, modern science has robbed it of the possibility to function as a place of mediation between it and nature, as a support of symbolic communication processes between the codes. As Kafka himself taught us, from that moment on every metaphor will be monstrous and socially unacceptable. He describes the transition in the story *In der Strafkolonie* with great lucidity. An aloof and neutral traveler is about to witness the last act of the colony's old judiciary regime, put in place by the previous commander, now dead, and observed by little more than a lone officer: with a complicated system of needles, a machine tattoos the words of the broken law onto the condemned man's skin, a long operation that ends with his death. However, as the procedure is falling into disuse and has practically run out of supporters, the machine is now dirty, damaged and no longer capable of functioning with its former precision. The traveler can't decipher the instruction manual, nor the complicated hieroglyphics needed to steer the movements of the machine's needles. Seeing that the machine doesn't work, the officer, driven to extremes, pauses the machine and takes the condemned man's place: in a tangle of components, the machine goes crazy, and the needles rip in to the officer's skin without writing a word. The usual transformation of the sufferer's body, the *"ecstatic expression"* produced when he begins to decipher the inscription in his wounds, and that the audience does everything to see, does not take place this time.

> [The dead man's face] was as it had been in life; there was
> no trace of the promised transfiguration; the thing that all
> the others had found in the machine; his lips were pressed
> together, his eyes were open, their expression was that of the

living man, and the point of the great iron spike had passed through the forehead.[24]

It is in this "tranquil belief" in a new phase, in the end of man's old privileges, in the lack of a superior point of view that legitimizes his place in the universe, that these questions, of which the cyborg is also the bearer, are inscribed.

24    Franz Kafka, *In the Penal Colony* ([1919] 1941).

[ 4 ]

# Spectacle, Sex, Death

Deirdre is a singer and dancer; Delphi a holovision star used to
make indirect advertisements (direct having been illegal for some
time) for her sponsor's products. Helva is a spaceship pilot, but
when it comes to choosing her crew "no actress on her opening
night could have been more apprehensive, more fearful, more
breathless,"[25] and her hobby, which gives the story its title (*The
Ship Who Sang*), is singing, something that, given her intellectual and instrumental prowess, she is capable of doing better
and with more versatility than any normal human. It appears
that authors of science fiction (in this case female authors)
have a fondness for linking cyborgs with the world of entertainment. This is no surprise if we consider the cyborg as a sort of
technological freak, and let's not forget that the playhouse, or the
circus ring, is this figure's homeland. Forever, the monster and
deformity (according to the etymology of the word) have been
judged worthy of being put on show. The cyborg exploits the
extreme, ultra-human possibilities of the body like the dwarf or

25    McCaffrey, *The Ship Who Sang*.

the bearded lady, which are comparable to those of the dancer or acrobat.

> For a moment everything was motionless upon the stage. Then, at the head of the stairs, where the two curves of the pillared balustrade swept together, a figure stirred. Until that moment she had seemed another shining column in the row. Now she swayed deliberately, light catching and winking and running molten along her limbs and her robe of metal mesh. She swayed just enough to show that she was there. Then, with every eye upon her, she stood quietly to let them look their fill […]. She stood quiet, swaying just a little, a masked and inscrutable figure, faceless, very slender in her robe that hung in folds as pure as a Grecian chlamys, though she did not look Grecian at all. In the visored golden helmet and the robe of mail that odd likeness to knighthood was there again, with its implications of medieval richness behind the simple lines. […] Now she swayed and came slowly down the steps, moving with a suppleness just a little better than human. The swaying strengthened. By the time she reached the stage floor she was dancing. But it was no dance that any human creature could ever have performed. The long, slow, languorous rhythms of her body would have been impossible to a figure hinged at its joints as human figures hinge.[26]

Here the freak turned horror into fascination, performing an exercise in seduction in the false but stimulating etymological sense proposed by Jean Baudrillard,[27] where the audience, expecting to see an artiste, first sees a machine, and then, as the show continues, a woman gifted with the most extraordinary talents. We also discern that Ms. Moore's entire description, considering the terms used, the evocative images, the atmosphere, quite openly suggest a religious event, or a sort of superhuman

26 Catherine L. Moore, *No Woman Born (1944)*.
27 See Jean Baudrillard, *De la séduction* (Paris: Galilée, 1979), 37: "Stratégie de Déplacement (seducere: amener à l'écart, detourner de sa voie)".

epiphany. In "developed" societies at the end of the century the show exculpated those same functions fulfilled by the dimension of holiness in previous eras. It is a "degraded" holiness, as Mircea Eliade would say: it doesn't conjure up any transcendent reality, but a sort of distracted unity amongst all the users, reconciled by mysterious electronic feedback processes that occur in the secrecy of the studios' production and recording equipment.

> The idea that art thrives on creative flamboyance has long been torpedoed by the proof that what art needs is computers. Because this showbiz has something TV and Hollywood never *had—automated inbuilt viewer feedback.* Samples, ratings, critics, polls? Forget it. With that carrier field you can get real-time response-sensor readouts from every receiver in the world, served up at your console. That started as a thingie to give the public more influence on content. Yes. Try it, man. You're at the console. Slice to the sex-age-educ-econ-ethno-cetera audience of your choice and start. You can't miss. Where the feedback warms up, give 'em more of that. Warm—warmer—hot! You've hit it—the secret itch under those hides, the dream in those hearts. You don't need to know its name. With your hand controlling all the input and your eye reading all the response you can make them a god.[28]

The show business world is also at the center of *The Continuous Katherine Mortenhoe* (or *The Unsleeping Eye,* 1974), a book by Englishman David G. Compton. In a world practically free of sickness and disease, a show about sickness and pain is one of TV's most attractive programs. NTV's *Human Destiny* is the best of this genre, and it is only natural that those responsible want to use one of their best reporters, Roddie. For the occasion, he has agreed to swap his eyes for a pair of miniaturized video cameras that transmit non-stop everything he sees at the television studios. The equipment can never be deactivated, and if Roddie

---

28   Tiptree, *The Girl Who Was Plugged In.*

closes his eyes or finds himself in darkness, excruciating pain will warn him that he must find new visual material for his system. In this way, the program will enjoy the immediacy and the truth of a live show (Bertrand Tavernier's *La Mort en direct*, 1980 *[Death Watch]* is based on this book). What the reporter must film are the last twenty-five days of Katherine's life. In charge of computer fiction for a major publisher (another aspect of the machine's entry into the world of entertainment and communication), she was found to be suffering from a progressive and incurable degenerative disease that leaves her with just four weeks to live. Compton returns to a theme already dealt with by American science fiction writers of the fifties and sixties (Bradbury, Sheckley): television as a "total" machine, as an inhuman mechanism that lives and prospers vampire-like on the emotions and pain of men, paying particular attention to the accuracy of the characters' speech and psychology, but above all with a highly acute awareness of their involvement in the entertainment system. As Ruggero Bianchi observed:

> ... the sense of the whole thing isn't in the fact that Katherine and Roddie are the victims of a system manipulated by the media against whom they attempt—successfully or unsuccessfully—to rebel, but in the fact that the two protagonists *belong* to the *media* world, taking part in it with every fiber of their being and, when the chips are down, they don't exist outside of it.[29]

Roddie's condition as a cyborg, on the other hand, is not unique to him alone: not only is it an obvious metaphor of the paroxysmal predominance of our social system's image, of the uninterrupted and circular process of production-consumerism-production image, but it also represents an effective mediation

29    Ruggero Bianchi, introduction to the Italian translation of David G. Compton's *The Continuous Katherine Mortenhoe*, ed. Nord, (Milan: 1977), III [trans. Robert Booth] (the introduction was not included in the 1993 edition); the U.S. title is *The Unsleeping Eye* (1975).

between machine and consumer. Thanks to the integration of body and television camera, he is capable of representing and of reinforcing the bond between the public and the visual system that is now the main guarantor of the "reality effect" on the entire globe. No matter how integrated he is with this system, however, Roddie maintains the more traditional needs of rationality that will take him to the final crisis. He is in fact convinced right from the start that the "truth" coincides with the "continuity" of the processes and especially with people:

> I had this thing about continuity, you see, having long ago decided that people were only true when they were continuous. As an attitude, an approach to my job as a reporter, it had done me very well. It had got me where I was at that moment [...]. It will be noticed that I was at that time very much concerned with what I saw as the truth.[30]

In fact, when on the screens he sees the transmission of the images that his eyes filmed sequentially, he realizes that the visual immediacy, what his eyes recorded, does not correspond in any way to what Katherine is in his mind, to how he "sees" her. Robbie resolves this conflict between an individual system of perceptions and affects and the social system of images and communication (a conflict evidently of an ethnic nature) by destroying the instruments linking his self to the social system; voluntarily surrendering himself to darkness, provoking the destruction of the miniaturized TV cameras, thus blinding himself.

This clearly Oedipal solution takes us back to a discourse present in the traditions of English literature on the inadequacy of senses, and particularly of sight,[31] but mainly to Freud's observations

---

30    Compton, *The Continuous Katherine Mortenhoe.*
31    H. G. Wells, in his *The Country of the Blind* (1911), describes a remote village whose blind inhabitants are convinced that the eyes of those who can see are the result of a disease, and have built a perfectly coherent universe that excludes sight. Borges and Casares, in their already mentioned *Los Immortales*, resume the theme of the creation of the super man through

 on the equivalence of blinding and emasculation,[32] formulated especially with reference to the myth of Oedipus. In fact Roddie is separated from his wife: their marriage destroyed due to his work as a reporter that therefore acquires a connotation of evident sublimity, reinforced by inserting video cameras in place of his eyes. When Roddie goes to visit her, during the course of the story, he refuses to make love with her. A disturbed condition in emotional relations, when not out-and-out sexual impotence, that often characterizes cyborgs or the "cyborgized." Smith's *scanners*, we have seen, tend to stick together because, when in the *habermans* state, humans find them almost unbearable, yet they must "cranch" whenever they want to have sex with their wives. Since his school days, Lucas Martino (the scientist in *Who?*) has turned his back on any sort of human relationship, preferring to concentrate on his schooling and scientific career, precluding in particular any possibility of satisfactory contact with a woman (though he doesn't approach the girls he likes, he will quite cold-heartedly establish a relationship with any other girl, a relationship he quickly becomes ashamed of and has no qualms about terminating): the "dehumanization" of which he will later be a victim is in some way anticipated in his past life. Roger Torraway, the lead cyborg of *Man Plus*, even has his genitals removed as "unnecessary" during the course of a complete body reconstruction that will allow him to live on Mars, and discovers that before being subjected to real castration he had already suffered metaphorical castration, because his wife systematically played around on him with a member of the same space crew (the woman's choice, as implied by the narrator, is not totally unrelated to the sort of obsessive relationship that Roger had established with her). This is with regard to the male cyborgs. As far as the female cyborgs go, quite a bit has already been said.

suppression of the senses, quoting English poet Rupert Brooke: "And see, no longer blinded by our eyes".

32    See Sigmund Freud, *Totem and Taboo* (1913) and *The Uncanny* (1919). The connection between the eyes and sexuality is also affirmed by Georges Bataille in *Story of the Eye* (1928).

Both Deirdre and Helva, for different reasons, have to exteriorize their femininity in a totally metaphorical and symbolic way, though no less intensely. Delphi and Burke, on the other hand, attempt a complete sexual relationship, but here satisfaction is conditioned by keeping Delphi's android nature a secret; the couple man/machine works only as long as the human part is kept hidden, revelation of the truth means the end of the male's love and the death of the cyborg, at least of the human part (Delphi, we are told, will survive with another female operator). The "mechanization" of man would allude, therefore, to the same inability to love that Otto Rank pointed out in the protagonists of those works based on the figure of the double, from *Dorian Gray* to *The Student of Prague*.[33]

Examined from this perspective, the cyborg is therefore presented as the objectification of a disturbed sensuality: not necessarily as a menace (on this point, attitudes vary from author to author), but certainly as a symbol, or catalyst, of an aggression against the individual or social "self" of which, however, the development of technology is an important component. All things considered, the Frankenstein syndrome returns to the fore, made even more disturbing by the fact that the attack on the man's identity, and especially his corporeal identity, does not come from the exterior, but straight from within his own body. Therefore, we will not be surprised if a large percentage of the tests examined in this chapter contain a more or less direct reference to the prospect of death. At times it is the cyborg's origin, connected to a fatal accident, that is averted thanks to this transformation of the man (*No Woman Born, Who?*); otherwise it is the cyborg who, when menaced, plans the man's death, even without realizing it (*Scanners Live In Vain*); or perhaps the cyborg's human partner, or its human half, die (*The Ship Who Sang, The Girl Who Was Plugged In, The Unsleeping Eye, Man Plus*).

33    See Otto Rank, *The Double* ([1914] 1989).

 The link between mental disturbance with strong sexual elements and death is achieved in a very interesting test presented by a "cyborg doctor" in Michael Crichton's *The Terminal Man* (1972). As is his wont, Crichton doesn't present his book as a story of science fiction, but as a fictional scientific report with graphics, photographs, precise references and dates, together with an extensive bibliography that makes a lot of sense, but is probably false in many ways. Benson, the protagonist, suffers from epilepsy, and during the attacks he becomes extremely aggressive, a condition that at times has taken him to the brink of killing people. The doctors, considering the trouble they have administering other therapies, decide to implant a microscopic stimulator in his brain, a microcomputer connected to the hospital computer via a radio link-up, the idea being to stimulate a certain area of the brain and prevent further attacks. Only psychiatrist Janet Ross feels any misgivings about the operation. Benson thus becomes a "terminal" man, as the surgeon explains somewhat coldly:

> Now, however, in this operation we have created a man with not one brain but two. He has his biological brain, which is damaged, and he has a new computer brain, which is designed to correct the damage. This new brain is intended to control the biological brain [...]. And therefore the patient's biological brain, and indeed his whole body, has become a terminal for the new computer. We have created a man who is one single, large, complex computer terminal. The patient is a read-out device for the new computer, and he is helpless to control the readout as a TV screen is helpless to control the information presented on it.[34]

Benson might not be the best patient for this kind of operation. His "personality disorders", that, according to the psychiatrist, are an integral part of his illness, include the conviction that "machines are everywhere. They used to be the servants of

34    Michael Crichton, *The Terminal Man* (1972).

man, but now they're taking over. Subtly, subtly taking over." 
His hate for machines has already extended to all those at the
service of machines, "mechanics, dancers, translators, gas-
station attendants," as well as those he already sees turned into
machines, "particularly the prostitutes." Benson escapes the
hospital, and the stimulator starts to break down, sending out
too many stimuli and putting the brain into a state of hyper-
agitation that provokes artificially produced crises. And so begins
the hunt for the patient who, in the meantime, has killed one of
the surgeons and the girl who helped him escape. Wounded and
hounded, in the hospital's computer room, it will be the psychiatrist, the only one who considers him a human being, a victim of
mistaken therapy, who will stop him with a pistol.

# 5

# Intelligent Machines

Benson's conviction that machines are taking control of our life is not new. In 1872, when in his book *Erewhon* Samuel Butler wrote the following, the hypothesis that machines had a "conscience" might still have sounded odd:

> There is no security against the ultimate development of mechanical consciousness, in the fact of machines possessing little consciousness now. A mollusk has not much consciousness. Reflect upon the extraordinary advance which machines have made during the last few hundred years, and note how slowly the animal and vegetable kingdoms are advancing. The more highly organized machines are creatures not so much of yesterday, as of the last five minutes, so to speak, in comparison with past time. Assume for the sake of the argument that conscious beings have existed for twenty million years: See what strides machines have made in the last thousand! May not the world last twenty million years longer? If so, what will they not in

the end become? Is it not safer to nip the mischief in the bud and to forbid them further progress?[35]

The scenario presented by Edward Morgan Foster in the story *The Machine Stops* (1909) is that of a completely artificial world in which man lives underground, totally dependent on food, rest and movement from a central machine in which automatic houses are the terminals. At the time, this world might also have seemed pure fantasy or considered excessively pessimistic. In the thirties, when Aldous Huxley wrote *Brave New World*, the material for judgement was already more abundant. The discussion that took place in 1984, the year that is the title of George Orwell's homonymous book, was criss-crossed with comments and forecasts on the real and possible development of machines in the informatics and telematics sectors. An American critic, Patricia S. Warrick, complained that, when dealing with robots and computers, the attitude of the vast majority of science fiction writers was one of pessimism and catastrophe.[36] One may argue the accuracy of this observation (after all, the most popular and best known author outside this genre, Asimov, represented the opposite view); but in any case one has to admit that the apocalyptic will exist as long as the integrated exist, and presumably this will last for some time to come. However, neither science fiction writers, nor analogous critics, will be responsible for curtailing the development of research based on sound economic trends. The swing between the opposite attitudes of excitement and denigration habitually present in the history of man is particularly accentuated in periods of transition, even more so if that transition is accelerated, convulsive and complex like the one initiated in the second half of the twentieth century. And from the moment the massive inclusion of machines into our daily lives brings with it, inevitably, an entire circle of enthusiasts

35    Samuel Butler, *Erewhon* (1872).
36    Patricia S. Warrick, *The Cybernetic Imagination in Science Fiction* (Cambridge, MA: MIT Press,1980).

and gullible *exaltés* of whatever is "new," a certain rebalancing of the trend is basically on the cards.

That reality transcends fantasy (by taking a different route to the latter because no one can honestly ask writers to act as prophets) is by now a common consideration, and just as well founded. The term "cyborg," as we have seen, was born in the shadow of NASA and space research. Even though the abundance of projects formulated in the sixties was reduced in the following decade, together with the entire space sector, the man-machine systems created from that research are, however, enough to leave the non-professionals flabbergasted. In the seventies, General Electrics' Cybernetics Anthropomorphous Machine Systems (CAMS) included mobile, manipulatory and multi-wheel vehicles, systems for telefactoring, all based on the principle of correspondence between the movements of an operator armed with a powered exoskeleton and a nearby, or more often distant, machine that repeats them, transmitting a sensory feedback (ponderous, spatial, tactile, sometimes even visual) to the operator. The machine's legs or arms thus benefit from the precision of the operator's movements, while the latter receives information directly from his senses and not from numerical systems (he feels the objects' shape or opportunely proportioned weight that the mechanical arms lift). Built by NASA, the Space-Horse systems gave analogous performances, and were made up of artificial limbs whose motors picked up electric signals from the brain, arms with tracking mechanisms directly linked to the eye that opened fire immediately.[37] This research was further developed in the eighties and nineties with virtual realities, and particularly with the "tele-presence" systems.[38]

These technologies were able to grow thanks only to the development of the computer. And thus it is man's new partner, his artificial other-half, keeping him company inside the cyborg. It

37    David M. Rorvik, *Brave New Baby* (1971).
38    On virtual reality, see chapter 7, "Technology under the Skin."

 is the new double, the one that today already rivals us in mastering situations that require laborious calculations, reductions of complexities, elementary decisions in the blink of an eye. What we foresee (and fear) may also rival us tomorrow in the activity that we have always thought rendered us unique in the world: thought. On one hand, there is the spread of the personal computer, machines still somewhat limited, that nonetheless perform tasks much faster and with greater precision than we do, while, on the other, the departure from restrictions placed on research into AI has contributed to modelling the imaginary in this direction. Naturally, there is nothing diabolical in personal computers, nor have researchers of AI ever led us believe, not even for the briefest of seconds, that their work hides a new race of machine suddenly capable of usurping man's prerogatives and his place on this planet. However, there is no doubt that this research has brought back the themes and classical problems of previously mentioned Western philosophical studies with regard to man's definition and place in the world, strongly influencing our imaginary too. This is true irrespective of the successes and failures that this discipline, on the borderline between informatics, mathematics, linguistics and psychology, has collected in less than sixty years of life (the starting date having been set at 1956). If we look at it from an informatics point of view, it is hard to contest that AI has succeeded in obtaining from computers performances that in a human being would be considered "intelligent", like playing chess, understanding text and being able to respond to questions on it, formulating medical diagnoses. But AI cannot boast of similar successes on the subject of cognitive psychology: intended as "simulation of the mind", like the attempt to reproduce the workings of the human brain in a computer program (naturally calibrated and chosen according to the particular mental activity to be simulated), it has not produced positive results, on the contrary, it has suffered more failures than successes. This is because AI machines "think" exclusively through the manipulation of formal symbols, according to a rational abstract model that is neither that of man, or animal.[39]

However, AI has made it considerably easier to solve problems. In criticizing the AI research program, starting with the debate kicked off by Searle in 1980,[40] philosophical positions are in general curiously inverted with regard to our somewhat naïve expectations. The most radical critics of AI, including Searle, have no "idealistic" or "dualistic" positions, so to speak, but are on the contrary strongly materialistic, and identify thought with the activity of the brain: this is why they find it inconceivable that "intelligence" may be attributed to something as immaterial as a computer program, no matter how complex it may be. Supporters of AI, on the other hand, appear little interested in the "metaphysical" question of material support for the intelligence processes, and concentrate on a so-called "functional" model of the mind, more alert to functions, to reactions, etc. In this sense, their attitude seems more in line with NASA doctors and engineers who, in the sixties, were the first to formulate a theory on space cyborgs. "I believe that life is more a question of relations and organization than one of material," Manfred Clynes declared.[41] It is clear that this view of the problem, one he considers irrelevant, rather than assume a precise position, the age-old dilemma of mind/body, seems better adapted to insure a peaceful integration of man and machine. From this point of view, the cyborg is a far less conflictive figure than it appears in literary works.

---

39    On the conceptual bases and story of AI, see Vittorio Somenzi and Roberto Cordeschi, eds., *La filosofia degli automi* [The Philosophy of the Automatons], (Turin: Boringhieri, 1986); and Roberto Cordeschi, *La scoperta dell'artificiale. Psicologia, filosofia e macchine intorno alla cibernetica* [The discovery of the artificial. Psychology, philosophy and machines associated with cybernetics] (Milan: Dunod, 1998).

40    The entire debate can be found in John R. Searle, "Minds, Brains and Programs," *Behavioral and Brain Science* 3, no. 3 (September 1980): 417–424.

41    See Rorvik, *Brave New Baby.*

  But there is another aspect to the study of AI that appears relevant to our debate, and this time more on the side of the imaginary than the philosophical, expressed or otherwise. It might be better to introduce it with an example. One of the more famous criteria used to decide a machine's "intelligence" is the so-called "Turing Test", which consists of submitting a series of tests (basically questions and answers) to the judgement of an outsider, data that comes from two interlocutors unseen by the judge, one a man, the other a machine. The latter passes the test if the judge fails to identify its answers in a significant percentage of cases. This image of a closed room from which comes information, answers, sheets of paper filled with words or images, acquires a significance that goes beyond the strictly scientific context used by researchers. It is something akin to watching television or working on a computer: the world of TV is flat and two-dimensional, while that of the computer is discreet, segmented, made up of numerous small, elementary movements, and atomic positions. It is perfectly normal that scientific work be carried out in this way, through abstraction and then the subtraction of the attributes of the objects to be studied. However, we cannot avoid shuddering, feeling a sense of unease, when the object of this study is our own mind. We cannot help contemplating with a certain detachment the segmented and quantized world of video and computer: all the more so if we see, even without desperation, that it coincides in a literal sense with the reality in which we live. And even more if we realize that the segmentation and quantization of the world becomes increasingly more like a fragmentation and a discontinuity of our own interior world, of a combination of activities that we usually call "self." If we look at things from this point of view, the cyborg changes its aspect, no longer an organic monstrosity, but more simply a combination of processes that occur between man and machine: already a daily experience, something that changes molecularly day by day. Seen as an indication of the existence and feasibility of the man/computer relationship, the cyborg becomes a linguistic problem: how to program the machine's languages and enrich

communications between man and machine; in other words, a
problem of interfacing. Yes, there remains a paradox, an unan-
swered question for the common conscience: that it is possible
that questions of "interpretation" are raised between the innate
language of man, that distinguishes him from other natural
beings, and the artificial language of machines, that man himself
created. That it is possible that a new creation is capable of telling
us more about the world than we already know ourselves.

Science fiction has long represented this paradox in dramatic
terms, speaking of the computer-generated reality that pits
itself against a purely human reality, or as the expression of an
evil plot against man (*The Computer Connection*, 1975, by Alfred
Bester), the thematic exemplification of the super man (*The Ring
of Ritornel*, 1968, by Charles Harness), the representation of man's
destiny of vicious slavery (*I Have No Mouth and I Must Scream*,
1967, by Harlan Ellison). But the more the computer becomes
a fact of daily life, the more the image of the "intelligent" and
"creator-of-reality" machine will be played down. For example, in
*Overdrawn At The Memory Bank* (1976) by John Varley, the figure of
the "man-trapped-in-the-computer", performed by Harness with
heroic overtones, is depicted in an everyday dimension, with a
touch of irony. The protagonist, attached to a computer following
a terrible accident, lives a personal decades-long experience in
just a few hours, in a fictitious and completely iridescent reality,
without being even remotely upset about it. The dwindling,
changing levels of reality bring to mind Philip K. Dick, but without
his grandiose and oppressive mood. When he returns to "reality",
the trapped man will retain fragments of his previous experience
in a tangible form, much like his university degree.

Taking his cue from the encounter between the human pilot and
the alien spaceship in the film *Star Trek*, Carlo Formenti describes
the process in this way:

> There still exists an indication, a difference: the creature has
> accumulated immense knowledge and it is now necessary

to repay a debt of information. This occurs in a totally new way: not through the human's resumption of control over the machine—not by redefining the skin of the Other, the place of separation and difference—but through voluntary union, clearly sexual, between pilot, second-in-command and machine. This union does not give birth to a superman or super-calculator, but to a super-cyborg that forces us to question ourselves on the place and the function of his skin, on the meaning of this metaphor, of this change. Here the theoretical story must be less rigorous, more allusive: the sensitive diaphragm that divides man and machine, assuming it still exists, can no longer be sought after in the productive process. The fact that society's indoctrination has developed way beyond that of material production is no accident: capital, as a system of simulation, takes on the work process only as one of the metaphors (perhaps not even the most important) of the development process. The general information-equivalent frees itself of productive referentialities, the stakes becoming the control of the language transformation process.[42]

This linguistic challenge that takes place on the borderline between man and machine tends to swing from material production to "immaterial" production. In the process of reciprocal interrogation between man and machine, projections and hitherto undreamed of exchanges arise, the machine no more humanized than man is mechanized. From productive investment to emotional investment. Luciano Gallino, a sociologist who, for a certain period worked closely with AI, proposing a model of the human mind (intended as "social actor") named Ego, and a model to interface with the machine, Alter Ego, both workable on the computer, concluded an exhibition of his work with these words:

42    Carlo Formenti, "La pelle della macchina" [The skin of the machine], *Alfabeta*, no. 17 [trans. Robert Booth].

A regular and prolonged interaction with systems that reveal, even in a limited sense, an intelligence on a par with human beings will surely end up changing something in the operator's mind. It is highly likely that, after a lengthy exchange with Alter Ego through Ego, the subject will no longer be the same, even in the relatively deep reaches of its structure. Obviously, interacting with non-intelligent machines is just as likely to modify personality traits. But interaction partnered with simulation, even if rough and limited, equivalent to that of a human being, assumes an intrinsically different nature. In some way indefinable and yet quite evident, it means interacting with a mind removed from its natural—I was about to say traditional—physi-ological support. It means interacting with systems that somehow show they possess a "self," an identity complex. It could be enough in some cases, because as far as the subject is concerned Alter Ego is a machine, whereas he is a person. Perhaps a new form of alienation; or rather a form of inter-action by no means original, a virtual symbiosis between two minds with different physical supports, from developments our current cognitive codes find quite indecipherable. Who says that a mind must be locked forever within a single brain?[43]

43    Luciano Gallino, *Mente, comportamento e intelligenze artificiale* [Mind, behavior and artificial intelligence], (Milan: Comunità, 1984), 74 [trans. Robert Booth].

# 6

# The Price of Immortality

Man's body is therefore mute. It could speak as long as nature spoke, and a series of secret, esoteric missives went from one to the other, and the repetition of rites illustrated the myth again and again, allowing the signs accumulated on the body to be deciphered. Today, nature no longer exists, it broke up into a series of delimited echo-systems, alternately threatened and protected, surrounded and made to emerge by an "ambience" that has taken nature's place, yet is completely artificial, as we know. The body spoke even if only to expound, at every given opportunity, on a supreme law that illuminated equally senseless facts and attitudes. But this law is now obsolete, the machine that wrote the articles went mad and killed the last custodian without even giving him the satisfaction of being able to offer his body as paper on which to write those articles for the last time. Death even threatens dwindling hope, the promise of one day having a system of equations, no matter how long and complicated, that tells us: "So from material comes thought, the bridge that from DNA arrives at the imaginary, dreams, speech." Philosophers today investigate the whys and wherefores that, in less than a century, have taken Western culture from a position of "strength" to one of "weakness," from "great stories" to fragments. It isn't the least relevant of the paradoxes that the era of technology's greatest expansion, namely man's capacity to modify the environment in which he lives with his artefacts, is the era that considers the crisis far deeper than the image man has created of himself, an image that was built (as some thought) to comply with the expansion of these capacities.

Until now we have tried to show how a figure of contemporary imagery, the cyborg, might illuminate, albeit with a tangential and oblique light, this complex of problems. The hypothesis that emerges, certainly in a very hybrid way, as suited to the argument, is that a part of the traditionally human prerogative, in keeping with the growth of its accomplishments, is being transferred to the machine; perhaps because this burden is becoming too great for its bearer. It is a process that brings both elation and fear, enthusiasm and pessimism, mocking advances and fearful retreats. In so far as it pertains to the argument that has been chosen, we attempted to document them all, without regard for either the pre-established thesis or the discriminatory parameters between the texts (for example the "literary" quality) that weren't essential to the illustrations of the indicated themes. Amongst these, one perhaps deserves a few more words. Man seems envious of machine's immortality. This isn't something new: man has always granted his more eminent creations the eternal life that he as an individual is denied biologically, and whose species' survival is by no means guaranteed. Nonetheless, even the great masonry and architectural creations, those that easily outlive their creators, are subject to a long and unrelenting decline due to the materials they are made of. Besides this, the remorseless passage of time and the linear approach even in this domain render death even more inevitable, without traditional correctives of a religious nature being able to call upon a significant course of action; despite contemporary thinking having dismissed death in a particularly radical way. The machine on the other hand seems to share in this linear temporality enough to guarantee a certain chance of survival: insofar as the advent of the computer distances its being from a material substratum and identifies with the "working principles" of an immaterial type, or largely independent of the support on which they are realized (the programs). The cyborg, this undoubtedly non-mystical union of man and machine, of natural and artificial, could therefore allude to the realization of man's age-old dream, "immortality."

Of all the characters in the science fiction genre examined thus far, one stands head and shoulders above the others, just as his author does amongst other authors: Palmer Eldritch, the "arcane pilgrim" in Philip K. Dick's *The Three Stigma of Palmer Eldritch* (1964). During the Kennedy and Vietnam War years, Dick combined an extraordinary capacity for analysis and the portrayal of contemporary American reality with an acute understanding of the deeper characteristics of the anthropological transformation that, for many, would only become apparent some ten years or so later. Palmer Eldritch is a very singular cyborg, anomalous with respect to all those we have analyzed until now. When he first appears in the book, his transformation is already complete: he arrives back from a mysterious voyage to Proxima Centauri, a red dwarf star of which nothing is known, other than it having involved him in an indeterminate accident. However, on his return his appearance is no longer entirely human: what is striking about the body is the artificial eyes, teeth and an arm, which will become a distinctive mark of his presence. He has come back with a very powerful drug named Chew-Z, with which he intends to supplant the drug already widely used by the settlers of Mars, Can-D, produced by industrialist Leo Bulero. A first stage of the book deals with this industrial fight between Bulero, a representative of the capitalist "old guard," and Eldritch, who fronts for the new breed of technological capitalists. At this stage it is already typical of Dick to reveal not the capitalists of the traditionally industrial sector, but producers and dealers of something popular with the masses like drugs, that render life tolerable to the terrestrials on Mars (an arid and squalid planet, far different from the one portrayed by Bradbury), projecting them into hallucinatory realities that make the settlers identify with protagonist dolls made of otherwise inanimate compositions. But, at the second stage of the book, Eldritch's Chew-Z doesn't limit itself to preferring (as might be interpreted) creations of the unconscious within preformed environments like the "compositions" of the dolls. The new drug, in effect, creates far more powerful hallucinatory elements, very real artificial worlds created by individuals without any reference to external stimuli, and in which other characters can be "trapped," as experienced by Bulero and his employee, Barney Mayerson, whom he sent to muscle in on the opposition. Gradually it emerges that these worlds are no more than variations of Eldritch's mental projections, like the "three stigmas" (artificial eyes, teeth, arm) that circulate amongst all the characters without their being able to stop it. Their appearance becomes the signal that the reality they are living at that moment is under Eldritch's control. Thus, as Darko Suvin points out, the three stigmas become "three signs of demonic artificiality. The prosthetic eyes, hands, and teeth, allow him—in a variant of the Wolf in *Little Red Riding Hood*—to see (understand), grab (manipulate), and rend (ingest, consume) his victims better."[44] But the cyborg here is not just the exponent of a change in an industry destined to better control and exploit its consumers within its system. It is also the symbol of an immortality attained through the manipulation of reality and time, a return of what is holy within the only dimension in which it is possible, the eternity and the pervasiveness of the merchandise's cycle: "I did not find God in the Prox system. But I found something better. [...] God [...] promises eternal life. I can

44    Darko Suvin, "*P. K. Dick's Opus: Artifice as Refuge and World View (Introductory Reflections),*" in Richard D. Mullen and Darko Suvin, eds., *Science-Fiction Studies. Selected Articles 1973–1975* (Boston: Gregg Press, 1976), 170.

do better, *I can deliver it,*"[45] Palmer Eldritch says. The religious dimension, armed with the industrial dimension of efficiency, becomes invincible. Behind the cyborg, and the anthropological upheaval which it delays, lives, as noted by Pagetti, a patriarchal obsession in which technological progress and return of the archetype is combined:

Leo Bulero and, later, Palmer Eldritch are father figures to Barney, the epitome of a paternity against which any form of rebellion is destined to fail [...]. On the other hand, both fathers are the result of a technological progress that turned them into monstrous creatures, cyborgs, disfigured faces that threatened the helpless and terrified children [...]. We are faced with the entropic condition of the Dickian universe and its message that by now is reduced to a single obsessive piece of information: the universe is Palmer Eldritch, Palmer Eldritch is the universe. Palmer Eldritch's three stigmas refer however to the devastating effects that the capitalist technology has had on mankind, to the exploration that man carries out in the shadow of a God-father halfway between childhood memory and electronic manipulation, to the fantastic representation of a journey of psychic regression.[46]

Literature's first monster in the modern sense, Frankenstein, was clearly the son of man; Palmer Eldritch, according to Pagetti's interpretation, incarnates the father. A possible sense of the journey taken by man's imagination and linked to technology is closed within this reversal of positions, despite not being completely spent. From son to father, from death to immortality. It all depends on the price.

45    Philip K. Dick, *The Three Stigmata of Palmer Eldritch* (1964).

46    *Carlo Pagetti, "Introduzione," in Philip K. Dick, Illusione di potere (Roma: Fanucci, 2009),* VI [trans. Robert Booth].

# THE POST-FORDIST CYBORG

[ 7 ]

# Technology under the Skin

In the popular imagination of the twentieth century, we saw the cyborg emerge as an ambiguous and grim figure: linked certainly to the developments of technology without which it would probably have failed to make it to the pages of science fiction books, to cinema screens, to comic books, but ultimately still immersed in a prevalently fantastic dimension that demonstrates ambition, concern, nightmares born from routine, but then immediately detached themselves in order to be projected into the "unreal" space of the imagination and, apparently, stay there.

## From the Imaginary to the Everyday

However, if we pay closer attention to the historic development of this figure, we notice that, starting in the sixties, it takes on a more domestic dimension, something closer to real life. The boxed brains from the stories of the twenties and thirties still have that metal robotic look, whereas Roger Torraway of *Man Plus* or Roddie of *The Continuous Katherine Mortenhoe* have an unmistakably human aspect, despite being modified by technology. The change is even more apparent if we think of cinema. Fritz Lang's intelligent intuition in *Metropolis* (1926), namely that the robot may look perfectly human, remained unique for a long time, and not until 1956 did it re-emerge in Don Siegel's *Invasion of the Body Snatchers*; but Jack Finney and Siegel's fake humans are extra-terrestrials, not artificial men. In order to celebrate his cinematic apotheosis, the humanoid robot (alias android, alias replicant, the indistinguishable copy of the original) found in Asimov's stories from the fifties, and Dick's a few years later, will have to wait until *Blade Runner* in 1982. The cyborgs of the fifties have a mien that, in general, makes them look very much like robots. In *The Colossus of New York*, for example, a 1958 film by Eugène Lourié, the brain of the scientist who dies in an accident is encapsulated in an imposing, clumsy and quite frightening metallic, vaguely anthropomorphic body, who must once again learn the basic movements and the fundamentals of speech (this mediocre film comes across as a boring copy of Whale's *Frankenstein*, with a tin body in place of the creature's monstrous fleshy body). But in the two cyborg films that better represent the eighties, James Cameron's *Terminator* (1984), followed by his *Terminator 2* (1991), and Paul Verhoeven's *Robocop* (1987), it is the human body that returns to the screen, in two very different but conspiring ways. Arnold Schwarzenegger's body in *Terminator*[47] is human only skin-deep: in the famous scene in which the cyborg (an android in reality) repairs its damage in a sordid hotel room, the camera reveals the inner workings of the body, such as the micro-video cameras in place of the eyes, the wiring and metal rods in place of the muscles and tendons in the arm. Cameron's fantastic technology was capable of enveloping a machine (the horrible metallic skeleton of the film's final scene when it rises up out of the flames to pursue Sarah Connor) with the faithful simulacrum of the human body, and the spectator, before the Terminator is

47     In reality *The Terminator* has a curious ancestry, also from the point of view of the plot, in Franklin Andreon's wild 1966 film, *Cyborg 2087*, in which Michael Rennie plays a humanlike cyborg from the future.

reduced to a (metal) skeleton, looks upon that merciless body, in all its hellish artificiality, as the image—the metaphor, also from an ethical point of view—of technology's invasion of the human body. The same invasion is shown as it unfolds in *Robocop*, which is the visual epitome of the authentic computerized electro-mechanical cyborg. The face of Police Officer Murphy (Peter Weller), who was almost killed in a gun battle against evil drug dealers, disappears for most of the film, buried beneath the solemn metallic helmet that hides his features, following the reconstruction process and the insertion of artificial components that turn him into a machine of law-enforcement (but the cyborg hangs onto a few vague memories of the human being he once was, so much so that the faithful Nancy Allen recognizes the supposedly killed-in-action cop beneath that mechanical façade); Weller's face reappears only at the end, in a scene exquisitely reminiscent of westerns.

By laying claim to the term "cyborg," Hollywood got it wrong from the start, making it a synonym of "android," but even so they somehow managed to register the new cultural and technological galaxy that allowed direct technical penetration of man's body. Both *Terminator* and *Robocop*, however, present extreme situations, both narratively and technologically (fantastic, hypothetic), necessary for the transformation of the body. These cyborgs can even frequent everyday life situations, offices, the homes of human beings, but their origins are still rooted in far-flung places in time, in space, in techno-science; the social character of that origin is still very indirect, very arbitrary. Going back to Stableford's classification, it is still all about medical cyborgs, adaptive cyborgs or functional cyborgs; or, if one prefers the terminology of Gray's manual, "restorative," "normalizing," "reconfiguring" or "enhancing" cyborg technologies.[48] But everyone knows that classifications exist to be refuted. In the

---

48    Chris H. Gray, ed., *The Cyborg Handbook* (London and New York: Routledge, 1995), 3.

 same year that *Blade Runner* was released, another cyborg hit the
screens, one that enjoyed less success, an absolutely new cyborg,
not even remotely akin to Hollywood (it could even be considered
anti-Hollywood), with a body whose technological integration was
by no means a deliberate choice, nor was it the result of surgery
or of a high-tech procedure: it was instead the result, more or
less spontaneous, but by no means less exceptional and sur-
prising, of a social process, of a particular configuration of the
communicative flow. In David Cronenberg's *Videodrome* (1982),
it is society, and in particular the social apparatus central to the
modernism of the media system that secretes the frightening
hybrid of man and machine, and produces it directly from
quotidian routine. This time the mixed dimension of anthropo-
technology isn't the result of a war between man and machine,
between past and future (*Terminator*), or from the collision/
collusion between criminal violence and institutional violence in a
desolated metropolis (*Robocop*), but from a clandestine, low-def-
inition television signal, the Videodrome, that impinges on the
ether between the other signals and so sends out psychic, more
profound images of particularly receptive individuals like Max
Renn (James Woods), the restless television producer always on
the lookout for increasingly more violent, more realistic porno-
graphic programs. With what was defined as "invisible editing",
void of "any magic or gothic atmosphere",[49] Cronenberg shows us
a world that is undoubtedly ours—even if to the nth degree—with
pervasive and morbid, but domestic television programming,
a constitutive element of our daily lives while at the same time
acting as a catalyst of pulses powerful enough to transform the
world around us, to wipe out every stable boundary between
the objective exterior and the interior of a psychic experience,
of sexual fantasies, of the urge to die. "The battle for the mind
of North America," says Professor O'Blivion, a sort of spirited
McLuhan to whom Cronenberg in some way entrusts the film's

49    Serge Grünberg, *David Cronenberg* (Paris: Editions Cahiers du Cinéma, 1992)
      [trans. Robert Booth].

philosophical bent, "will be fought in the video arena, with the Videodrome. The television screen is the retina of the mind's eye. Therefore, the television screen is part of the physical structure of the brain. [...] Therefore, television is reality, and reality is less than television[50] While Max turns into a "hallucination machine",[51] the world around him also changes, without the spectator ever being able to decide whether or not this transformation depends on Max's altered mind or if, within the film's world, it has an objective quality: the videocassettes originating from Videodrome become agitated and shake before being slipped into the video recorder, the television screen becomes soft and expands, dilates, Nick's lips (the radio diva who pulls and ferries Max into the world of Videodrome) no longer create a flat image, but extend into the room, enveloping and absorbing the pro-tagonist. With Nick having become an element of Videodrome, almost without realizing it, his body begins to manifest the stigmas of the cyborg. A hole opens up in his stomach into which he slips the videocassette that will trigger the process of trans-lation: later, from the same hole, Max will pull out a viscous pistol of organic fluid soldered directly to his hand with which he will avenge those who tried to change him into a pawn for their game. None of this is the result of a mission carried out by some human or mechanical agent. Cronenberg doesn't show us any specific technology responsible for this transformation: it happens before the eyes of the spectator, spontaneously, even though obviously shocking, the direct "effect" of television. The fusion of Max's hand with the pistol takes place within his body, in a process that the screenplay doesn't worry about explaining, and the result is an image linked much more to the organic of cinematographic and comic-book cyborg traditions. It is because Max Renn

50    Cronenberg, *Videodrome*.
51    Grünberg, *David Cronenberg* [trans. Robert Booth].

 appears to escape the standard cyborg categories that I suggested he be defined as a "media cyborg" or "coded cyborg."[52]

The hybrid figure, as we know, is one of the central figures of Cronenberg's cinema. The fact that the hybridization man-machine (namely the cyborg) is one of the Canadian filmmaker's favorite themes was confirmed with, apart from *Crash* (1996), his next film *eXistenZ* (1998). *eXistenZ* picks up, just over fifteen years later, where *Videodrome* left off (this time with more explicit and insistent references to Philip K. Dick): for those involved, the slide between the "real world" and the virtual worlds is impossible to distinguish. Except that this time television is no longer the medium that creates this slide, but is instead centered (understandably so, seeing that the film was made at the end of the nineties) on videogames. However, as always with Cronenberg, the theme of virtuality is not present at a purely dreamlike level, with the sole representation of the altered perceptions that signal the entrance into parallel universes generated by the various media. From *Shivers, Rabid and Brood* to *Dead Ringers* and *The Fly*, Cronenberg's attention is constantly focused on biological processes as the origin, the means, the organizational center, and battlefield of the imaginary. As in *Videodrome*, Max Renn's body bears the visible and traumatic signs of his entry into the new dimension (the television, in the powerful end scene, explodes revealing an interior of blood and entrails), so eXistenZ is an artificial, but live game, Game-Pod, made up of synthetic meat, MetaFlesh, that comes into direct contact with the player's nervous system via a connector plugged into his spine at waist level, the Biosport. This "connection", fired from a special pistol, looks just like a sexual orifice (as on other occasions with Cronenberg: Rose's armpit-vagina in *Rabid,* and the long scar on Gabrielle's leg in *Crash* with which James makes love). And so the player, in order to play the game, must become a modified,

---

52    Antonio Caronia, *Il Corpo Virtuale* [The Virtual Body], (Padova: Muzzio, 1966), 91–92 [trans. Robert Booth].

reconfigured human being, must accept an organic artificial presence inside his body, and must be in symbiosis with Game-Pod: he must become a cyborg, despite being organic and not electro-mechanical.

## Universes to be Kept in the Pocket

Already in 1982, therefore, *Videodrome* shuffled the cards in the cyborg's universe and signaled, somewhat before its time, a change in the imaginary relative to the relationship between man and machine. There is a scene in the film that, seen years later, proves to be singularly prophetic: at the headquarters of the company that produces Videodrome, Max is made to wear a helmet with which the technicians may study his hallucinations. But the editing and the visual structure of the scene somehow suggest that the helmet is more than just an image "recorder", that it is almost a go-between through which Max evokes and visualizes his sadistic fantasies about Nick. In 1982 the term "virtual reality" was still relatively unknown, but when, some years later, one began to see—first at fairs and specialized conventions, then at videogame halls, hospitals, research centers— the head-mounted displays, Cronenberg's fans will remember that scene with pleasant amazement. The technologies capable of simulating artificial environments that go under the heading of "virtual reality"[53] had in effect already taken root back in the sixties and seventies, thanks to the work of researchers like Ivan Sutherland (inventor of the head-mounted display), Alan Kay, Nicholas Negroponte and others, at institutions like the Architecture Machine Group (known later as Media Lab) of MIT, and Atari Laboratory. The basic intuitions are credited to "visionaries" like Douglas Engelbart and J.R.C. Licklider, whose idea of a "man-computer symbiosis" influenced the widespread



53    See Howard Rheingold, *Virtual Reality* (New York: Summit Books, 1991), and Sandra K. Helsel and Judith P. Roth, *Virtual Reality, Theory, Practice and Promise* (*Westport,* Meckler, 1991).

 use of the personal computer. Between the late sixties and early seventies, Myron Krueger, an experimenter whose work bordered on technology and art, had already created interactive environments that reacted to the movements and actions of visitors, the most famous of which (1975–77) was "Videoplace". Krueger had chosen the name "artificial reality"[54] for these environments, a term that was not successful. But it wasn't until the mid-eighties that a genius self-educated twenty-five-year-old named Jaron Lanier put together Sutherland's helmet, Thomas Zimmerman's "data glove" produced for NASA—a Lycra glove that duplicated the movements of the hand—stereophonic sound and a new visual programming language in order to build the first environment that would be called "virtual". The founding of his company, the Visual Programming Language (VPL), coincided with the brief but intense boom of virtual reality that kept journalists, commentators and crowds of curious people all over the world busy for five or six years. In the intentions of its prophets, virtual reality had all the characteristics of a new interface between man and computer; an interface that no longer needed sequences of letters numbers or abstract symbols to be typed on a keyboard, nor two-dimensional icons to be dragged across the screen with the mouse—all replaced by simple movements of the body. The software that created the reality (the reality engine) responded to movements and changed the environments around us (walls, furniture, objects) to make us perceive them as those of an ordinary reality. The computer-generated virtual world brought to us via the small screens and the helmet was a copy of the real world, or one that abided by different laws, but appeared to sight, sound and, within certain limits, touch (if one wore the data glove) as the real thing: one could pick up virtual objects, move them around, hear the accompanying sounds; one could move from one virtual room to another, or stay outdoors, walk barefoot across virtual grass beneath a (virtual) bright blue sky.

54    Myron W. Krueger, *Artificial Reality II* (Reading, MA: Addison-Wesley, 1991).

The creation of a world that shared numerous characteristics with the real world, and in which the participant had opportunities to do things unheard of in the real world (like being able to fly by simply lifting a finger, or being endowed with superhuman strength) was what mainly caught the public's imagination; in fact for some years the biggest money makers were the "immersive" videogames. The moment the user put on the helmet or the gloves (or gripped the joystick) it became a temporary cyborg in a man connected to a machine, in an "augmented human being" (*augmented reality* was another term suggested to indicate virtual reality), and took off for worlds hitherto unknown. Not necessarily a fantastic world, also a world reminiscent of the one lived in every day (except for the scale of the objects and the ranges that made up the surfaces, but this was a problem of the computer's power). For the first time, cyborg technology involved *sensorial* translation—and no longer a purely *imaginary* one—in a parallel reality. As with Cronenberg, the technical transformations (even temporary) applied to the body influenced the environment in which the body was immersed, the world. The creators of the more lucid virtual realities were aware that this leap forward in exteriorization (a modality always founded in technology, but capable this time of a greater quality) implicated a rethink of the concept of experience. It's worth knowing what Lanier had to say in a 1989 interview:

> Virtual reality is not like the next way computers will be; it's much broader than the idea of a computer. A computer is a specific tool. Virtual reality is an alternate reality [...]. In Virtual Reality your memory can be externalized. Because your experience is computer-generated, you can simply save it, and so you can play back your old experience anytime from your own perspective. Given that, you can organize your experience and use your experience, use your externalized memory in itself, as the basis for what you would call The Finder in the Macintosh. That will be quite a different thing.

   You can keep whole universes in your pocket or behind your ear and pull them out and look through them any time.[55]

Virtual reality's mass media boom died out like a meteor, just in time to anticipate a far more consistent (and apparently more durable) boom, that of the Internet, and yet that togetherness of technology appears to have broken the promise of giving everyone "entire universes to keep in one's pocket". In reality it's not like that. Pending an ulterior increase in computer power, and equipment less awkward than the now ancient head-mounted display and the data glove with their mass of cables, technology continues to modify our bodies while doing the same to the world around us. And it continues to mix the real world with its virtual image, multiplying the informative channels open between man and man, and between man and environment. The cell phone alone is an instrument that connects us to the whole world (and the whole world to us, which isn't fun seeing how anyone can follow our every move if they so wish) in a way that wasn't even contemplated until a few years ago. However, in the usual labs at the Massachusetts Institute of Technology, the future, as a lazy journalist would say, advances by giant leaps and bounds. The consortium's "Things that think" projects include numerous "softwear" research programs: glasses with miniature cameras that show a constant picture of what is going on above and behind us (with the added capability of changing the luminosity or perspective of our surrounding world) without us having to turn our heads; a live keyboard to take notes; sensors in the shirt or pocket that measure our heartbeat, how fast we are walking, even how much we sweat. "Three forces," wrote Neil Gershenfeld, the co-director of the *Things That Think* consortium, "are driving this transition: people's desire to augment their innate capabilities, emerging technological insight into how to embed computing into clothing, and industrial demand to move

55   Adam Heilbrun, "Virtual Reality. An Interview with Jaron Lanier," *Whole Earth Review* (Fall 1989): 112.

information away from where the computers are and to where the people are."[56] Going in the same direction is the "Personal Area Network" (PAN) invention by IBM's Tom Zimmerman that utilizes the very small electric current that courses through our skin to send messages from one part of the body to another, or from body to body (so that, for example, one could pay with a credit card without producing it, by simply shaking hands with the vendor).[57] In other words, cyberspace can exit the computer screen or our heads to become our daily space, and reality loses its objective character more and more to become a technological artefact; much like our body, and the body of the cyborg.

## A Fractal Subject for a Fractal World

So there you have it, cyberspace: because a unifying word was needed, one that could indicate the new space inhabited by the cyborg, deal with the graphic simulations of virtual reality, of "augmented reality" filtered and enriched by the "softwear," or by the more immediate and domestic version that is the Internet's "non place." This expression came from a novel, the first by an American writer, who lived in Canada, wrote science fiction stories and for many years believed there was "something" behind the computer screen, something that not even he could identify (considering the fact that little was known about computers at the time), a sort of virtual space in which some of his characters could enter and leave as they wished. He named it matrix in his first stories. In *Neuromancer*, published in 1984, the term juxtaposed with cyberspace. The word was liked not only by readers, but also by scientists and technologists, and rapidly began to be used to indicate not only the literary invention, but also the environment of virtual realities, and then that of the Internet. William Gibson was the most gifted (quickly

---

56    Neil Gershenfeld, *When Things Start to Think* (New York: Henry Holt, 1999), 47.
57    See Antonio Caronia, *"Contanti o Stretta di Mano?"* [Cash or Handshake?], *Virtual*, no. 38 (January 1997).

 becoming the most famous) of a small group of writers who, as occasionally happens in the world of science fiction, wanted to revamp the genre, to reconnect it somehow to its origins as a "hard" technological genre, but speaking—with a little extrapolation—more of the present than of the future. The success of *Neuromancer* brought international recognition to this group of writers, who, thanks possibly to the word cyberspace and to highlight their attitude as "angry young men", were baptized "cyberpunks" by the critics. The cyberpunks, because of their predilection for mirrored sunglasses, preferred to be called the "Mirrorshades Movement", and were all the rage not only at book conventions, but also at scientific and cultural conventions exploring virtual reality. And the neologism that defined them was soon adopted by radical and libertarian groups from U.S. and international countercultures that had for years intervened on the social use of technology.[58]

The cyberpunk writers' great innovation consisted in knowing how to *see* the changes in the relationship between technology and society, over and above the arrangement of the *existing* imaginary, in understanding and describing the turning point in technology's effective, triumphant, dramatic, ironic, but in the final analysis everyday entry to body technology, and the gigantic, subterranean transformation in the ways of producing values in society that rendered them possible thanks to this technological revolution. They knew how to describe, with drama and irony, this new aspect of society that in just over ten years had become a common experience, but one that between 1980 and 1985 was still relatively unheard of, and was only intuited by those who for years had frequented certain film and literature circles, or by those who stubbornly reflected on the whys and wherefores

---

58    See *Cyberpunk. Antologia di Testi Politici* [Cyberpunk. Anthology of Political Texts], ed. Raffaele Scelsi (Milan: ShaKe, 1990). A reconstruction of the literary and social aspects of that movement may be found in Antonio Caronia and Domenico Gallo, *Houdini e Faust. Breve Storia del Cyberpunk* [Houdini and Faust. A Brief History of Cyberpunk], (Milan: Baldini & Castoldi, 1997).

of the defeat of the anti-capitalist struggle in the sixties and seventies. During those years, many of us were stunned by the spread of Thatcherism and Reaganism, and still took it, instinctively, to be a sign of continuity with the capitalistic reconstruction of the previous phases, as the instrument to kick-start the accumulation process and to reconstitute, in a "classical" way, the profit margins of businesses. Instead, Gibson, Sterling and friends showed us, with a certain understatement, that what was starting was a new model of accumulation, that capitalism and society were reinventing themselves, that the relationship between the political, economic and social institutions, of the traditional capitalistic society had been shaken, that the relationship between territory and power was changing, that new relations between new institutions were springing up; that a new geography of power, of command, of relationships between individuals and society were emerging in the new areas of *virtuality*, and inextricably linking information, communication, knowledge and production. Perhaps not with the same clarity for all, but these—and we can say so today—were the reasons for the very real enthusiasm that gripped many of us in Europe between 1985 and 1987 when we read *Neuromancer*. Driven by this enthusiasm, we rushed out to look for books by Gibson's friends: Bruce Sterling, Rudy Rucker, Lewis Shiner, John Shirley and others, starting with that old Urania of 1981, *City Come A-Walkin'* by Shirley, in which the city, like an organism in symbiosis with its inhabitants, fought to defend itself against the aggression of the new "model of development".

In 1986, Bruce Sterling effectively summarized this transformation of the social imaginary in his introduction to *Mirrorshades*, the group's *anthology-manifesto*:

> Science fiction, at least according to its official dogma, has always been about the impact of technology. But times have changed since the comfortable era of Hugo Gernsback, when science was safely enshrined, and confined in an ivory tower. The careless technophilia of those days belongs to

a vanished, sluggish era, when authority still had a comfortable margin of control. For the cyberpunks, by stark contrast, technology is visceral. It is not the bottled genie of remote big science boffins; it is pervasive, utterly intimate. Not outside us, but next to us, under our skin, often inside our minds. Technology itself has changed. Not for us the giant steam-snorting wonders of the past: the Hoover Dam, the Empire State Building, the nuclear power plant. Eighties tech sticks to the skin, responds to the touch: the personal computer, the Sony Walkman, the portable telephone, the soft contact lenses.[59]

"When authority still enjoyed a comfortable margin of control." Sure, here Sterling ducks the question of dominion with great elegance, seeming to almost legitimize the misunderstanding that the decentralization and the territorialization of command (the end of the "comfortable margin of control") signify a decrease in conflicts in post-Fordist society. Naturally, this isn't true, on the contrary the contradictions in the new methods of capitalist production are sharpened, and not alleviated, by the new levels of integration, by the squandering of classical political intervention, by the direct subsumption of language in the productive process. But this doesn't do away with the fact that the intuition was singularly and deeply just. There is no longer any possible control (in the classic sense) when technology abandons a specialized and separated sector of the community, and becomes a constitutive element of daily life; by directly entering the body it literally creates "life". Less than ten years later, in 1994, Kevin Kelly, guru of the new technologies and new economy, renewed this concept, starting with the title of his monumental and documented review on the "new biology of machines", *Out of Control*.[60] The era of electro-mechanics has definitely run its course,

---

59    Bruce Sterling, "Preface," in *Mirrorshades: The Cyberpunk Anthology*, ed. Bruce Sterling (Gettysburg, PA: Arbor House, 1986), xiii.

60    Kevin Kelly, *Out of Control. The New Biology of Machines, Social Systems and the Economic World* (Reading, MA: Addison Wesley, 1994).

whereas that of biomechanics has just started. The integration of information control in new generation machines relieves them of a predictable and strictly deterministic dimension, of increasingly identical and repetitive behavior, making them more and more akin to living beings, capable in some way of "resolving problems." of establishing strategies of adjustment to the world, rather than living in limited worlds tailored to fit their limitations.

> In the coming neo-biological era, all that we both rely on and fear will be more born than made. We now have computer viruses, neural networks, Biosphere 2, gene therapy, and smart cards – all humanly constructed artefacts that bind mechanical and biological processes. Future bionic hybrids will be more confusing, more pervasive, and more powerful. I imagine there might be a world of mutating buildings, living silicon polymers, software programs evolving off-line, adaptable cars, rooms stuffed with co-evolutionary furniture, gnatbots for cleaning, manufactured biological viruses that cure your illnesses, neural jacks, cyborgian body parts, designer food crops, simulated personalities, and a vast ecology of computing devices in constant flux.[61]

William Gibson, whose antennae are always sensitive to picking up suggestions that circulate in cutting edge technology and society, did not hesitate to discuss many of these things with us, for example "mutating buildings": one of the most impressive inventions in his novel *Idoru* (1996) is that of a post-earthquake Tokyo rebuilt by biological nanotechnology that assembles the ruins and reconstructs the buildings as living beings, buildings that "slid apart, deliquesced, and trickled away, down into the mazes of an older city."[62] As for "simulated personalities," we need only frequent any one of the virtual communities that for decades have flooded the telematic networks in order to collect examples of the plentiful "self" fragments that make up the virtual subjects,

---

61    Ibid., 500–501.
62    William Gibson, *Idoru* (1996).

 and that weave a canvas of "individual" narrations to which only the particular, often marginal characteristics of physical subjects correspond; subjects and virtual narrations that, in the simulative dimensions and relational hypertrophy of the networks, find an environment wonderfully suited to their expansion, an environment that protects their fragility and weakness, extolling instead their hybrid character, lying between the real and imaginary.

To get back to Baudrillard's formula: what happened, why this "breakdown of imaginary over reality"? How could this migration of technologies from fantasy to effectuality create such blatant effects in the reconstruction of reality, in the contamination of imagination and behavior, and in the breakup of traditional combinations (work/spare time, private/public, trivial/cultural)? Where does this invasion of parallel universes throughout our daily activities, mechanisms and social processes come from? Let's hypothesize; go back to the figure of the cyborg. What occurred during the eighties wasn't just that applying technological fantasies to the body, limited to vague potentials at the best of times, started out as shaky, fitful laboratory experiments before going on to become increasingly more solid technologies that could be bought for a steal on every street corner. Gradually, as this took place, it became clearer that the technological imagination (science fiction, and more) had seen, or foreseen, the phenomenon in too limited a way, in a single direction: it had imagined (desired or feared) an invasion of the body, a rush for the *exterior* to intrude on the *interior*. Conversely, while this certainly took place, a movement in the opposite direction also occurred: the *interior* invaded the *exterior*. What until yesterday had occupied man's psychic and private dimension, his fantasies and dreams, withdrew from that secret dimension, became immediately communicable, could be shared with others far beyond the linguistic instrument, could become a common experience. Until now these experiences had existed only within the traditional mediation of accepted and established social behavior, for which fantasy, dreams and idle digression were the hidden rear zones that contributed to propping up the front line of a "personality" considered presentable, because it was different, the labyrinthian and dark basements that fed, in somewhat unconscious ways, the image that everyone had of themselves, the one that they presented to the world. In principle, everything could now be objectified, "represented," brought to life; the technologized body brought a whole world with it, an environment in which to prosper, express itself, grow and become stronger. And if this was possible, it means that the dogma of reality's uniqueness faltered: the break-up of "self" brought with it the plurality of worlds. The parallel universes left the pages of science fiction, or the quantum physicists' most daring cosmological hypotheses, to become the worlds of the house next-door, from which one could come and go in a relatively "normal" fashion. In one of the more acute reflections on cyberpunk science fiction, Brian McHale explained why it (and, more in general, all of science fiction) is such an appropriate instrument for this type of theme. According to McHale, science fiction (much like the postmodern novel) enjoys an "ontological dominance", whereas the modernist novel (and the thriller) worries instead about epistemological problems. "Epistemologically-oriented fiction (modernism, detective fiction)," McHale writes,

> is preoccupied with questions such as: what is there to know about the world? Who knows the world, and how reliably? How and to whom is knowledge transmitted, and with what degree of reliability? The questions typical of ontologically-oriented fiction (postmodernism, science fiction) are instead like: What is a world? How is a world constituted? Do alternative worlds exist, and if they do exist how are they constituted? What are the elements that distinguish different

worlds and the different types of world? And what happens when one goes from one world to the other?[63]

Now "poetry in which the category 'world' is plural, unstable and problematic, seems to imply a model of 'self' that is also plural, unstable and problematic." But while postmodern story-telling represented the disintegration of "self" at the language or narrative structural level, and not the *world* of fiction in which the narration is set (with some shining examples, like Pynchon's *Gravity's Rainbow*), cyberpunk science fiction has chosen a more direct route, "that of rendering effective, literal, what in the postmodern poetic appears as a metaphor with regard to the language, the structure, or the materiality of the means. Where postmodernism uses a figurative representation of dis-integration, cyberpunk texts generally project fictional worlds, which include (fictional) objects and (fictional) phenomena that embody and illustrate the problems of individuality: human-machine symbiosis, artificial intelligences, biologically-engineered alter egos, and so on.[64]

If we take a look, for example, at *Neuromancer*, we see that it contains in effect a far wider and quasi exemplary range of such characters and situations of the sort, and that the interactions between these characters serve to define what could be called the "ontological consistency" of the worlds amongst which the action unfolds. There is a typically "traditional", electrome-chanical cyborg, Molly, a female samurai with a prosthetic body: mirrored glasses in place of the eyes, retractable blades beneath the fingernails. There is the new mass-media cyborg, Case, who abandons his own inert body on the chair, with the faithful Ono-Sendai on his lap, in order to romp about between the "lines of lights in the non-space of his mind, amassed and constellated

63    Brian McHale, "Elements of a Poetics of Cyberpunk," in "Postmodern science fiction," special issue, *Critique: Studies in Contemporary Fiction* 33, no. 3 (1992): 139.

64    Ibid., 149–150.

with data" of cyberspace, "a consensually-lived hallucination 
experienced daily by billions of legitimate operators.[65] There are
artificial intelligences like Wintermute and the one that gave its
name to the book's title, Neuromancer, packed with software
that, though lacking human "motivation," could be considered a
"personality". And there is even an immaterial individual, Dixie
Flatline, a "constructed", with the thoughts, conscience and ability
of a cyberspace cowboy, now dead, recorded on a silicon platelet.
To get a better understanding of how the relationships between
these characters help link their different worlds, the different
levels of reality that co-exist in *Neuromancer*, the more interesting
scenes are perhaps those in which Case, by way of a *simstim*
transmission switch (cyberspace's "commercial" version), can link
up with Molly whenever he wishes and see the world through
her senses. McHale analyses these scenes from the point of view
of the characters' innovation, pointing out that this automatic
switch of point-of-view is "a subversive gesture, implicitly under-
mining the model of the centered centripetal self upon which
modernist perspectivism rests":[66] for example when through
Molly's eyes, Case contemplates himself huddled with the cyberspace deck between his legs. But in these scenes there is also an
implication, so to speak, on the nature of the world. During the
combined attack on Sense/Net's headquarters (in the second
part of *Neuromancer*), carried out by Case from cyberspace,
by Molly from inside the building, and by the gang of Modern
Panthers wreaking havoc on the city's communication system,
Case's continuous passage from one environment to another (his
room, cyberspace, the Sense/Net building), with the trouble he
has distinguishing "his" sensory input from Molly's, explicates
the world's already disparate and no longer monolithic character.
It is a scene that summarizes *Neuromancer's* implicit ontology
(and cyberpunk fiction in general): the world is no longer made
up of just one physical environment, of a "nature" transformed

65    William Gibson, *Neuromancer* (New York: Ace, 1984).
66    McHale, "Elements of a Poetics of Cyberpunk," 158.

 by man's material presence (buildings, streets, cities), but rather a plurality of levels—not only material, but imaginary and informative too—that intertwine and intersect, in which the characters may live again and again, and simultaneously in certain cases, and in which it is not possible to establish a hierarchy, so that a (for example, material) level may become more "established" than others. Rather, the game between the levels and the handling of the plots that weave in and out of each other constitute the cyborg era's real, new form of politics.

Evidently, such a world is neither controllable, nor cognizable—not even in principle—with the completeness and rigor required by the thought of modernity. In it, the cognitive and interpretive models applied by man cannot keep the necessary distance from the objects that they are supposed to model or represent, but inevitably end up becoming elements of the game, parts of the world, hybrid objects that must model themselves. The anthropologist may not deem his presence within the tribe as an element that does not influence the behavior of the observed. The physicist cannot simultaneously determine the position and extent of movement of the subatomic particle that he is studying. There is no algorithm capable of automatically generating all the theorems of arithmetics. In the cyborg era the traditional program of classical science, the Laplacian dream of knowing the world's past and future based upon a thorough examination of its state at any given moment, is abandoned: recognizing the unmanageable complexity of the world—not only "natural", but also technological—one may concentrate on the objective of reproducing numerous new versions of that complexity, of repeating the characteristics of the physical and social macro-cosm in the microcosm of every single machine and micro-universe that surrounds it like a bubble. It is no longer the moment for theory and critical thought, it is the time for simulations. "To think" no longer means to formulate theories, but to produce operative models, simulations. The cyborg is a fractal subject, hybrid not only in its body, but also in its rapport with the world.

# 8

# From Electromechanics to Genetics

## Problems of Classification

In his rich dictionary of artificial and fantastic beings, Vincenzo Tagliasco defines the cyborg in a way that appears more reductive with respect to the chosen criteria in this book, but does, however, come substantially to the same conclusion: that artificiality is now the characteristic that distinguishes our body. His meticulous taxonomy provides a continuum of 36 categories that go from "normal" human ("being born from female bearer following sexual intercourse") to "human simulators" (mannequins, inflatable dolls and the like), listing all the possible categories in terms of quantity and quality, and of artificial interference with the body. Tagliasco sandwiches the cyborg (category 10) between mutants and cloned beings. He starts with the definition in the Zingarelli dictionary ("Cyborg: human being onto which mechanical and electrical organs have been grafted," which is somewhat reductive), to then declare:

> In the present taxonomy the cyborg is given a somewhat restrictive interpretation, linked to evaluations of

performance and not to the substitution of so-called "normal" functions through technical and technological solutions. Within the ambit of such significance a human being who has undergone the substitution of various joints— hip, knee and elbow—or the transplant of the cornea, heart, lung and liver, must not be considered a cyborg [...]. Whereas, a human being who entrusts himself to neuropharmacology to strengthen his intellectual prowess could be considered a cyborg, inasmuch as the component of pharmacological artificiality alters his machine-brain.[67]

Given that "evaluations of performance" is a reasonably elastic conception, and that it could include "substitution of functions"— considering it means to bolster a performance that has fallen below accepted levels—it must follow that potentially every human being, in developed societies, is a cyborg. And the final example would confirm this conclusion. On the other hand, talking about the prospect of genetic programming on already chosen offspring, Tagliasco asks: "Is it about introducing artificial elements in natural processes, or about acknowledging that the so-called 'natural' presents rules of evolution profoundly correlated to the technological development of the human com- munity?"[68] It is here that all the ambiguity of "normality" emerges, along with the recognition that, within the realms of human activity, each overly definite distinction between "natural" and "artificial" risks leading to irremediable contradictions. With each technical advance, each new prosthesis, each new manipulation of physiological and relational mechanisms that guarantee new performances, the imaginary reacts by attributing the character

67　Vincenzo Tagliasco, *Dizionario degli essere umani fantastici e artificiali* [Dictionary of fantastic and artificial human beings] (Milan: Mondadori, 1999), 156 [trans. Robert Booth]. With regard to the precision of taxonomy— that touches on the maniacal at times—and the wealth of references to books, stories, films, comic books, TV series and technological achievements, this work represents an irreplaceable medium, not only at the Italian level, but also internationally.

68　Ibid., 15–16.

of "natural" to the technologies of the previous generation, labelling these last objects as nostalgic memories.

The fountain pen was so beautiful, elegant and fluid before the squat and noisy typewriter came along to mechanize an activity as magical and intimate as handwriting. But immediately after that it was so great to pound away on a typewriter before the advent of the computer: I could feel the resistance of the key to the pressure of my finger, I had to feed and remove the sheet of paper from the roll, it felt so alive, not this impalpable machine. And then the longing for natural medicines, and the cultivation of organic foods to save us from the pollution of "overly" industrialized and technologized products. Just or understandable solutions, clearly, if the previous technologies turn out to be polluted or harmful, but to which do we grant with exaggerated generosity the qualification of "natural", without reflecting on the fact that basically it is just a recourse to different technologies: in an industrial or post-industrial world it is always "more" and not "less" technology that allows us to realize what is considered by common naivety as "natural".  So, while inspecting the impact of technology on man and his body, we must highlight the cyborg's technological and social leap, and its continuous relationship between body and technique that is constitutive of our species, as indefinite, "open to the world", and thus in need of an "action" that modifies the original nature, starting with that of the body.[69]

However, Tagliasco's planning and, even more, the example he gives of neuropharmacological enhancement are useful points because they take us back to the origin of the debate on the cyborg in the early sixties, when, as mentioned earlier, New York doctors Manfred Clynes and Nathan Kline took part in research

---

69    Here I refer to Arnold Gehlen's philosophical anthropology, expressed for example in *Der Mensch. Seine Natur und seine Stellung in der Welt* [*Man, his nature and place in the world*] (1940), and *Urmensch und Spätkultur* (1956). In Italy, Gehlen's approach was expanded by Ubaldo Fadini (see for example his *Principio metamorfosi. Verso un antropologia dell'artificiale* [Milan: Mimesis, 1990]).

to modify the body in order to render it better adapted to space travel. This research was not born from nothing. From a certain point of view it fit very nicely into the same mix of psychology, biology and physics from which the studies on the theory of servomechanisms were born in the forties and fifties and that, according to the neologism proposed by Norbert Wiener, would be called "cybernetics:" studies that used the new mathematical theory of information elaborated in the same years by Claude Shannon and Warren Weaver, and based upon the premise that a single theory (based on the principle of retroaction, or feedback) was capable of registering the physiological behavior of animated organisms as well as that of automatons.[70] How much of that research program, later to be included in the field of AI, turned out to be well founded and fruitful is obviously another question (which we tried somewhat briefly to allude to in chapter 5). Recently, at the United States Archives, Thomas P. Hughes dug up a 1950 document that could be one of the first cyborg telematics emergencies (in a broad sense, naturally). It deals with a "Progress Report" from the scientific branch of the United States Air Force, dated 1 May 1950, in which, amongst other things, it mentions:

> The aerial defense system (ADS) reveals points in common with all the system types listed in the *Webster's Dictionary*. But more particularly it enters into a specific systems category: the category of organisms. This word, according to the Webster's, means "a complex structure of interdependent and subordinate elements whose relations and properties are largely determined by their function on the whole." The emphasis is placed not only on the configuration and on the

---

70 See Roberto Cordeschi, "Quarant'anni di indagini meccanicistiche sulla mente: dalla cibernetica all'intelligenza artificiale" [Forty years of mechanistic inquiries into the mind: from cybernetics to artificial intelligence], introduction to Vittorio Somenzi and Roberto Cordeschi, *La filosofia degli automi: Origini dell'intelligenza artificiale* [Philosophy of the automatons: origins of artificial intelligence] (Turin: Bollati Boringhieri, 1994).

disposition, but also on what is determined by its purpose, 
an attribute that for the ADS represents an advantageous
characteristic. The ADS is therefore an organism [...].
But what are organisms? There are three types: animate
organisms, that include animals and animal groups, mankind
included; partially animate organisms, relating to animals
associated with inanimate mechanisms, as in the case of the
ADS; and inanimate organisms, like vending machines. These
organisms all have in common sensors, decisional centers,
action adjusters and actuators or executive agents. The
organisms also have the power to develop and to grow [...].
On top of that, they demand to be supplied with materials.
[...] Almost all organisms can discern not only the external
world, but also their own activities [...]. The organism's
function is to interact with the activities of other organisms
and to modify them, usually to achieve a specific goal.[71]

What is interesting here, other than attributing the same
characteristics to the "systems" as those of living organisms, is
the hint of a sort of "collective cyborg:" the entire air defense
system is supposedly a "partially animated organism." However, it
is a relatively short step from "associating animals with inanimate
mechanisms" to conceiving permanent mechanical appliances
within the human body. This is precisely what Clynes and Kline
did in 1960.

However, an examination of their treatise written that year, *Drugs,
Space and Cybernetics*, reveals that the cyborg the two scientists
considered of a particular type was in fact far different from the
one illustrated by science fiction in books, comics and the cinema.

71    *"Progress Report of the Air Defense Systems Engineering Committee,"* May 1st
      1950, written for the scientific convention, American Air Force Chief of Staff,
      George Vallee Committee, C50-10788-AF; quoted in *"Modern and Postmodern
      Engineering,"* report by T. P. Hughes at the seventh annual Arthur Miller con-
      ference on science and ethics, MIT, April 8th 1993 [retrans. Robert Booth].
      I owe knowledge of this paper to the courtesy of Mario Orlandi of the Uni-
      versity of Pisa, and to Paolo Alberti.

122   The merit goes to Sadie Plant for having revealed and reflected upon this incongruence so we'll let her guide us.[72] In fact, it is true that Clynes and Kline thought of inserting a mechanical device into the body, a pump capsule triggered by osmotic pressure, but it was supposed to effect "slow and constant injections of an active biochemical substance, at a biologically comparable speed".

> The treatise (by Clynes and Kline) dealt with the possibility of a drug conforming to an organism's metabolism, to its capacity to transform food and liquids, to its zymotic system, to its vestibular function, to cardiovascular control, to maintaining muscular tone and the perceptive abilities. It also dealt with ways of regulating sleep and the hours awake "through the use of those types of drugs recognized with the name of psychic energizers, combined with other medicinal drugs" already in use. It listed problems categorized by such phenomena as variations of pressure and temperature, of radiation, of magnetic fields and of gravitational force. It discussed methods for combatting psychoses and for alleviating the effects of "perceptive immobility and lack of action" that the space traveler might have to face, reflecting on the techniques for causing unconsciousness or oblivion in extreme emergencies and suffering.

Therefore it has to do, as Sadie Plant says, with a "chemical interface":[73] an approach to the cyborg problem that would have had the merit of revealing, once again, the continuity of this new figure (planned or imagined) with procedures of "chemicalization"

72   Sadie Plant, "Soft Technologies for Soft Machines: the Chemical Interface," *Virus Mutations*, no. 6 (1999), from which come all the quotes of the next paragraphs [retrans. Robert Booth].

73   The broader meaning with respect to the informatics with which Plant uses the term "interface" is analogous to the one given it by Pierre Lévy in *Le tecnologie dell'intelligenza. Il future del pensiero nell'era dell'informatica* [The technologies of intelligence. The future of thought in the computer era], (Verona: Ombre Corte, 2000).

of the body already amply carried out during the history of man, 
and now in line with the new technological possibilities. But that
is not how it went.

> This chemical interface is one of the richest zones in which
> to reveal the cyborg's emergence. By wiping out the confines
> between man and machine, between natural and artificial,
> between intimate and distant, between bodily interiors and
> exteriors, the drug-induced cyborg overcomes the limits with
> greater intensity than the successive drug-free models. But
> no matter how this fundamental document has classified
> the drug as a determinant characteristic of the cyborg, it
> has not succeeded in influencing the debate that developed
> later. The theme linked to the effects of pharmaceuticals was
> developed in several books concerning the cyborg, including
> *Metrofaga* by Richard Kadrey, *Snow Crash* by Neal Stephenson
> and *Neuromancer* by William Gibson. Furthermore, over the
> past years, both medical and military practices, as well as
> the illegal use in cities, have produced such a proliferation
> of narcotics, addicts and methods of administration that the
> chemical interface today constitutes one of the technical
> changes to which the most sophisticated, inquisitive and
> profound of men is subjected. But whereas the role of
> artificial organs and other types of even more extraordinary
> prostheses have had enormous importance in recent discus-
> sions on the cyborg theme, the chemical interface stands out
> instead because of its absence.

In recent years, researcher Sadie Plant, who studied global
politics on drugs and their effects on the social imaginary, has
tried to explain the absence of this subject from debate, "that
rendered it impossible to say where exactly the human ended
and where the cyborg began," by resorting to politics' increasingly
repressive attitude towards drugs since the start of the seventies. "The silence that descended on their cyborg (Clynes and
Kline's)," she wrote, "is a clear indication of how the climate of
prohibition induced by the war on drugs has spread insidiously

124   at the more general level. [...] The war on drugs, launched with the aim of regulating the chemical composition of individuals and collectivities, demands the control of every aspect of the research and development of these substances, their production, distribution and consumption." And she continues reconstructing, albeit summarily, a story about the taking of psychoactive substances, in peacetime and especially in wartime, that goes back to at least the Spanish conquest. Plant ends by reaffirming the role of drugs, "soft technology for soft machines," in the constitution of the body's self-perception as a chemical machine, but reveals the slippery nature of this figure of popular imaginary, and, behind the removal of the chemical interface, glimpses a normalizing choice analogous to that of the creation of the drug addict (a figure who, as we know only too well, was an effect of the fight against drugs, and not the cause, as the prohibitionists claim).

> If we admit to the existence of a cyborg population, then it lives in this pharmaceutical zone: but in truth this hypothesis is very problematic. Even when cyborgs are discussed in relation to more visible technological prostheses, to object that the term seems overly redundant is far too predictable, inasmuch as human beings have always been, in one way or the other, cybernetic organisms. From the point of view of a chemical interface, this conclusion becomes even more inescapable. Cyborgs have always been elusive, and drugs have rendered them practically impossible to define. Initially, cyborgs could have been defined as a precocious interest for the biochemical self-regulation system, but once they fell prey to Hollywood screenwriters and to academic debate they became far more definite, they were turned into more austere entities that worked toward a confirmation rather than a challenge, somewhere between human and mechanical. Just as the category *drug addict* at the end of the nineteenth century contributed to concealing the fact that "sober" individuals were as dependent on chemistry

as those taking drugs, so it was that the *cyborg* at the end  of the twentieth century served to classify, limit and stem a combination of practices, experiments and explorative interventions that turned men into soft machines as much as they did cyborgs.

## The Body as Interface

It could therefore be said that the electromechanical variant of the cyborg has found its true function within a "discursive strategy" (to use a Foucauldian concept) meant to define and harness a figure and practices that institutions would otherwise find unmanageable. Let's try to get a better understanding of how this could have happened. There is no doubt that the figure of the man-machine hybrid, present in American science fiction since the twenties as a variant of the robot, has since the sixties progressively gained visibility, not only in the new fictitious conquest of space, but also in relation to a series of transformations (at the time only incipient) by the productive structure, by technologies and by the capitalist organization of labor. The idea of an intimate collaboration, of a combination between organic and inorganic is in certain ways born from the closeness with the machine achieved in capitalistic industry, with the worker's subordination to the rhythms and demands of the machinery introduced by Taylorist labor organization. However, as long as we remain within the bounds of Taylorism–Fordism—and of electro-mechanical and mechanical industrial technologies—the machine is not only an autonomous power, it is also free and opposed to man: "In handicrafts and manufacture, the worker makes use of a tool; in the factory, the machine makes use of him,"[74] or rather "[t]he *instrument of labour*, when it takes the form of a machine, immediately becomes a *competitor of the*

---

74    Karl Marx, *Capital: A Critique of Political Economy; Vol. 1* (Harmondsworth: Penguin in association with New Left Review, 1976), 548.

 *worker himself.*"[75] The possibility of interpenetration, of a very real symbiosis, however conflictive and dramatic, between man and machine, occurs only with the existence of technologies far more ductile and flexible than their electromechanical counterparts, namely those that are computerized and digital. These technologies, especially towards the end of the seventies when, with the invention of the personal computer, they escaped the logic of industrial "gigantism" and began to develop their own potential ductility, flexibility and immediate adherence to market changes, allowed capital to take a huge leap forward in the processes of socialization of work and of molecular penetration in the productive processes in every aspect of daily life, rendering the processes of valorization incomparably more complex with respect to classic capitalism, and narrowing the gap between work and spare time, creating the conditions for an ever increasing globalization pushed as much by the economy as by the new processes of self-valorization. This is the new constellation of the production and the imaginary to which the name of post-Fordism has been given.[76]

In a first phase, the imaginary registers this change and reacts by simply breaking up and remixing the already known and available elements. Even when it is electromechanical, the cyborg immediately relates to a relationship between man and machine that is changing, alludes to a proximity to man and machine that first reveals the changes in the machine's dimension, logic and functions, and then the inevitable changes that these processes induce in man. But the process, however intuited, is still not fully developed, and the imaginary's previous traditions of modernity on which the new imaginary works are all still centered on elements of heavy artificiality (metallic bodies and prostheses, machines and engines): these are therefore the components

75    Ibid., 557.
76    For a general introduction see Adelino Zanini and Ubaldo Fadini, eds., *Lessico postfordista. Dizionario di idee della mutazione* [Post-Fordist lexicon. Dictionary of ideas on mutation] (Milan: Feltrinelli, 2001).

found again in the electromechanical cyborg. However, we 
have already seen that different elements are present in these
traditions, more "biological" with respect to the crystalized ones
found in the figure of the android or robot, to which the cyborg
is closely related; one just has to think of the alchemical figure of
the *homunculus*, or the mix of electricity and bodies with which
Mary Shelley creates the Frankenstein "creature". But so that this
alchemical-chemical-biological imaginary may fully redeploy itself
in the cyborg image, new elements are required, new changes
in the scientific paradigms, in technologies, in the analysis of
society. The first of these elements is surely the emergence of the
"information" concept initially in cybernetics and then in biology
with the new centrality of genetics. The basis of this new point
of view was the discovery of the DNA helix by James Watson and
Francis Crick in 1953, but it took another twenty years before
molecular biology learned to work with Shannon's concept of
"information, and until, as much in science as in the imaginary,
it could develop the idea of a living being as an organism of
elaboration and distribution of information. The second central element is not only the appearance of new technologies of
information and communication, but is principally their detailed
diffusion throughout society: not so much the birth of informatics
as a discipline at the end of the forties and fifties, more the
appearance of "distributed informatics" following the invention
of the personal computer—an invention, it's worth remembering,
that did not stem from the lecture halls of higher education or
from the laboratories of industry, but from the thick of political
movements and anti-authoritarianism and the Californian
underground movement of the seventies.[77] The third element
is the change of the social model that evolved internationally
during the course of the seventies, the assertion of a "method of
production no longer dominated by forms of vertically integrated
accumulation and the distribution of contracted wealth between

77   For a rich and prompt reconstruction of this event, see Steven Levy, *Hackers:
     Heroes of the Computer Revolution* (New York: Dell/Doubleday, [1984] 1994).

 collective and supervised representation of the State, but by forms of flexible accumulation capable of integrating, of networking ways, times and places of production, one more different than the other: from the robotized factory to the hi-tech farm, from the industrial district to the Mexican *maquiladora*, to the days of global finance."[78] The link between information, communication, knowledge and production in post-Fordist capitalism determines a crucial change in our discourse, what Christian Marazzi called "the linguistic turn of economy:"

> Of all the characteristics brought to light in recent years to explain what distinguishes *just-in-time* production strategy from Fordist production strategy, what would appear more effective for the study of political and socioeconomic transformation is the one placing *communication* at the center of technological-productive innovation. One might say that the combination of just-in-time strategy, communication and flow of information gains direct access to the productive process. Communication and production overlap in the new method of producing, whereas in Fordism the communication era juxtaposes with the productive process.[79]

This superimposition of communication and production has, amongst its various consequences, this, fundamental to our analysis: that the body, our principal instrument of communication with the world around us, our global interface, is directly integrated into the process of capitalistic development, "fulltime" so to speak, and also integrates with technology in a far

<hr>

78    Adelino Zanini and Ubaldo Fadini, "Il catalogo è questo" [The catalogue is this], in *Lessico postfordista*, 11. A brief and effective description of this new phase of capitalistic production can be found in Part II of David Harvey's *The Condition of Postmodernity: An Enquiry into the Origins of Cultural Change* (Cambridge, MA and London: Blackwell,1990).

79    Christian Marazzi, *Il posto dei calzini. La svolta linguistica dell'economia e i suoi effetti sulla politica* è [The place of socks. The linguistic shift of the economy and its effects on politics] (Bellinzona: Casagrande, 1994); subsequently published by Bollati Boringhieri (Turin 1999), 14.

more pervasive and delicate way than in the past. And since both 
production and development today are far more integral and
extensive linguistic processes than they were in the recent past,
so language today traverses our entire body, and the structure
according to posture, rhythms and technologies that the Fordist
industrial era did not know. Here is another meaning of Sterling's
slogan about technology that works its way "under our skin
and inside our minds." In the eighties, the transformations in
the process of the production and circulation of goods began
to be transcribed directly and very visibly onto man's body: the
fusion of man and technology realized through the hybridism
of the body can therefore tell us new stories, not only about the
body-cum-factory, like Asimov's robots and Dick's replicants, but
also like that of the body-cum-television as in *Videodrome*, like
that of the body-cum-information-cum-simulated worlds as in
*Neuromancer* or *eXistenZ*. And today, the cross between man and
technology can even avoid resorting to the invasion of foreign
bodies, transferring the full weight of artificial insertion onto the
modification of the information apparatus, with an external and
programed involvement in the genetic code. The real leap into
the cyborg dimension, therefore, will no longer be in a "chemical
interface," but more likely a "genetic interface."

## Biopolitical Devices

This new immaterial invasion of the body created by language
naturally brings with it a series of new problems and opens new
conflictual configurations in post-Fordist society. On the one
hand it highlights an entire biological, "corporeal" dimension of
politics, whose rulings are no longer limited to subjecting the
body to a disciplinary regime (and the jails and prisons, at times
camouflaged to look like "hospitality centers," are increasingly
more reserved for bodies of foreign extraction, for immigrants
still refused citizenship), but instead give technology the job of
improving the behavioral patterns now granted bodies, with a
relatively higher "tolerance". This political investment in bodies,

however, on the other hand dangerously reduces their autonomy by putting pressure directly on the linguistic device: the
body risks being unable any longer to pit speech against that
extralinguistic residue that is visible and almost ostentatiously
present in face-to-face oral communication, and that in writing
remains hidden instead, but produces subtle and veiled effects,
especially when it maintains a poetic dimension or is anyhow
oriented towards the expressive aspect of communication. It is
that residual aspect of the body with respect to speech that was
expressed with such force, even if in a cryptic way, by Artaud
in his plea to the "body without organs," and that Deleuze and
Guattari picked up again some decades later to make it one of
their more charming "borderline practices."

There is no doubt that the general picture is the one already out-
lined by Michel Foucault in his research on the history of sexuality
when he identified, at the origin of modernism, the change from
having the "right of death" to a power that intervenes positively
on life: "the ancient right to *take* life or *let* live was replaced by a
power to *foster* life or *disallow* it to the point of death."[80] It is the
emergence of bio-power, or of bio-politics.

> For the first time in history, no doubt, biological existence
> was reflected in political existence; the fact of living was no
> longer an inaccessible substrate that only emerged from
> time to time, amid the randomness of death and its fatality;
> part of it passed into knowledge's field of control and
> power's sphere of intervention. Power would no longer be
> dealing simply with legal subjects over whom the ultimate
> dominion was death, but with living beings, and the mas-
> tery it would be able to exercise over them would have to
> be applied at the level of life itself; it was the taking charge
> of life, more than the threat of death, that gave power its
> access even to the body. If we can apply the term *bio-history*

80 Michel Foucault, *The History of Sexuality: Vol. 1: An Introduction,* trans. Robert
Hurley (New York: Pantheon Books, 1978), 138.

to the pressures through which the movements of life and 
the processes of history interfere with one another, one
would have to speak of *bio-power* to designate what brought
life and its mechanisms into the realm of explicit calculations
and made knowledge-power an agent of transformation of
human life [...].[81]

The devices of bio-political power that appear at the start of the
new century, during the cyborg era, seem however to go beyond
both the categories identified by Foucault, that of the *"anatomo-
politics of the human body"*, namely the disciplinary integration
of the individual's body within the systems of social control, and
the *"bio-politics of the population"*, in other words the combination
of measures meant to regulate the biological macro-parameters
of the communities (birth and death, health conditions, etc.).[82]
Linguistic investment in the body does in fact seem to delineate,
against the background of these two mechanisms that self-
perpetuate with a minimum of explicit intervention (the breakup
of the social state), a process of coordination of the bodies with
the social imaginary of dimensions never seen before. With the
extension of the process of appreciation within society and no
longer just at "production locations" in the strict sense (factories),
post-Fordist capitalism in fact appears capable of profiting from
every spatial and temporal modulation of the body, from the
imaginary's every articulation, from social energy's every pro-
vision, even uncontrolled—from shopping malls to discotheques.
Whatever language the bodies speak, there is always the risk of
it becoming a dialect of a new language that speaks through us
even when we believe we are outwitting it. For this reason Big
Brother was able to abandon the "control room" of political power
(if it ever truly lived there) to become a TV format that only the
most naïve of us consider to be an innocuous farce. At the end of
the seventies, Foucault was still able believe that the unleashing

81    Ibid., 142–143.
82    Ibid., 139.

    of the plurality of bodies could effectively withstand the debate on power:

> It is the agency of sex that we must break away from, if we aim—through a tactical reversal of the various mechanisms of sexuality—to counter the grips of power with the claims of bodies, pleasures and knowledges, in their multiplicity and their possibility of resistance. The rallying point for the counterattack against the deployment of sexuality ought not to be sex-desire, but bodies and pleasures.[83]

Today, when a bio-political perspective can no longer take life as a *given* on which to build its own macro- and micro-regulative operations, when the body is assailed by languages, not only imaginary but also by techno-science, and is subordinate to an actual production process, how can we still hope to work on a "tactical reversal" of languages? Does the mix of biology and technology, in which the cyborg's body has been transformed, perhaps not rob us of every possibility of rescuing it from the apparatuses of power that operate on both the imaginary and the symbolic? Donna Haraway, with courageous and almost mocking determination, suggests that the only way to avoid being swallowed by the post-Fordist wolf is to throw yourself at it, to fully embrace the artificial perspective and to play the card of hybridity and impurity that it offers us. "This chapter is an effort to build an ironic political myth faithful to feminism, socialism, and materialism. Perhaps more faithful as blasphemy is faithful, than as reverent worship and identification. [...] At the centre of my ironic faith, my blasphemy, is the image of the cyborg," she declares in the opening of her *Cyborg Manifesto*.[84] She goes on: "I am making an argument for the cyborg as a fiction mapping our social and bodily reality and as an imaginative resource

83    Ibid., 157.
84    Donna Haraway, "A Cyborg Manifesto: Science, Technology, and Socialist-Feminism in the Late Twentieth Century," in *Simians, Cyborgs, and Women: The Reinvention of Nature* (New York: Routledge, 1991), 149.

suggesting some very fruitful couplings. Michael Foucault's biopolitics is a flaccid premonition of cyborg politics, a very open field."

What's in this "open field"? Firstly, the "confusion of boundaries", Haraway says. She indicates three fundamental cessions that are at the base of the cyborg condition: the lines between animal and man, between organism and machine and between physical and nonphysical have all been violated. These boundary cessions that took place with the direct influence of science and technology with regard to social relations create fluctuation and uncertainty in traditional identities (for example, "feminine" identity), that today become transitory and fluid, and must be constantly negotiated with communications technologies, and life.

> Communications technologies and biotechnologies are the crucial tools recrafting our bodies. [...] Technologies and scientific discourses can be partially understood as formalizations, i.e., as frozen moments, of the fluid social interactions constituting them, but they should also be viewed as instruments for enforcing meanings. The boundary is permeable between tool and myth, instrument and concept, historical systems of social relations and historical anatomies of possible bodies, including objects of knowledge. Indeed, myth and tool mutually constitute each other.[85]

In fact "the cyborg is a kind of disassembled and reassembled postmodern collective and personal self, the one that feminists must code". This fluid, test vision of society and the relations it produces between its members, and between those members and their objects of knowledge and intervention, is what allows Haraway to see conceptual categories and practices of intervention in constant movement, and not in a frozen static nature. And therefore allow the new "cyborg subjects" to insert themselves in the joints between the concepts and modular

---

85    Ibid., 164.

 protocols that define the world in order to overthrow, even locally, this movement's leadership and to impose new relations, new knowledge, new practices. To overthrow the "informatics of domination" in the pleasure of living. If we must no longer talk of organisms, but of "biotic components," if the strategies of control concentrate on interfaces and not on the "integrity of natural objects," if "any component can be interfaced with any other," then it is these processes of communication and passages of information that make up the biopolitics of the twenty-first century, and not a clash between identities well-defined or otherwise. Talk always starts with a location, with a situation, with a condition, with a body, there is no disembodied discussion, no absolute and no clear-cut point of view. Our knowledge is always "situated knowledge." And if, in order to reconstruct Haraway's discourse, I reduce to a minimum the references made on the condition of women and the internal debate on feminism from which that discourse was born, it isn't to ignore these determinations or to strip them of their "bias;" on the contrary, it is to show that only a reflection originating from a historically determinate condition, one that is aware of this, may produce "exportable" indications and effective methodologies for the comprehension and involvement of reality.

The key point of Haraway's discourse on cyborgs is that the processes of hybridism with technology exonerate the bodies and subjects from the need to relate to a "founding myth," to a yearning for a collective or individual identity. The myth of one's origins isn't just about capitalism and patriarchy, it's also about antagonism in the progress toward modernity. "Feminisms and Marxisms have run aground on Western epistemological imperatives to construct a revolutionary subject from the perspective of an oppressive hierarchy and/or a latent position of moral superiority, innocence and a greater closeness to nature."[86] But the cyborg has no "origins;" it is a fluid and experimental element

86    Ibid., 176.

in constant mutation. This is where its strength lies, in its being unfamiliar with the myth of language transparency, in its ability to speak a language rooted in its body without having to refer it to a presumed native dimension, in maintaining within a language that extra-linguistic and corporeal trace that the informatics of domination tends to eliminate.

> Cyborg politics is the struggle for language and the struggle against perfect communication, against the one code that translates all meaning perfectly, the central dogma of phallogocentrism. That is why cyborg politics insists on noise and advocates pollution, rejoicing in the illegitimate fusions of animal and machine. […] Without the original dream of a common language or original symbiosis promising protection from hostile "masculine" separation, but included in a text that lacks a definitive privileged reading, a history of salvation, to recognize "oneself" as fully implicated in the world frees us of the need to root politics in identification, vanguard parties, purity and mothering. […] Cyborg imagery can suggest a way out of the maze of dualisms in which we have explained our bodies and our tools to ourselves. This is a dream not of a common language, but of a powerful infidel heteroglossia. It is the imagination of a possessed feminist who manages to strike fear into the circuits of the super saviors of the new right. It means to both build and destroy machines, identities, categories, relationships, space stories. Though both are bound in the spiral dance, I would rather be a cyborg than a goddess.[87]

Donna Haraway's "bodily, literary, figurative, non-metaphorical" theory (as defined by Rosi Braidotti in her introduction to the Italian edition) is thus at the service of a political project: the rebirth of a radical and socialist feminism. But it is well rooted in a complex and articulate vision of relationships between science, technology, society and bodies: rapidly changing relationships

87    Ibid., 181.

  in which it is not possible to guess a "direction," only a "field structure." Where the Frankfurt School's tired followers saw only impending destruction and catastrophes and death's inescapable victories, Donna Haraway was capable of seeing contradictions, trials, conflicts: a whole field of possibilities. Perhaps the moment has come to start an inquiry into how this concept of "possibilities" came about in late modernity. This is what we will attempt to do in the next (and conclusive) chapter.

# 9

# Cyborg Ecstasy

The twentieth century was the century of the possible. This claim can be interpreted in numerous different ways, all linked to each other: as always, philosophers do not reflect on an unchangeable abstract world, but on the historical reality that surrounds them.

From the point of view of what's been done, in human experience the area of the "impossible" appears to have gotten progressively smaller. More than in any other era, the last century saw technology accomplish things considered quite impossible in previous centuries: from human flight (including the one against the planet's gravitational attraction) to transmissions via ether or cable of images and data, to the manipulation of genetic codes. Yes, man did indeed aspire to such things, or at least he tried to. The difference consists in the fact that although man aspired to such things and not being possible at that time in history, they were transferred to worlds and dimensions separate from daily experience. With regard to myth (Greek myth, being one of the foundations of western civilization), divine beings fly, project their simulacra onto battlefields, and mate with humans to create offspring that are half-man and half-god. But when a man,

 Daedalus, invents flight, his son crashes, and on this hypothetical technology it's as though a ban was declared. Despite the life of man, once separated from the gods, life's suffering was lessoned thanks to the miserable knowhow like fire and metallurgy, the price was high nonetheless: the heathen Prometheus, chained to a rock in the Caucasus, and his liver, gnawed daily by Zeus's eagle. Over a long and torturous journey through the centuries, the blooming of a new technical era from (to use Mumford's term) a paleo-technical one transformed the status of these myths into everyday experiences. But why is it that today Icarus's wings do not melt in the sun, while poor Prometheus's liver continues to be eaten by the eagle?

From the point of view of thought, the burgeoning of new and previously unheard of possibilities has ended up causing the notion of what is necessary to falter. Matter has evaporated into components to which our senses have no direct access, and whose behavior does not correspond to that of sensible objects; and the only way in which thought can think of them is to have recourse to mathematical instruments that need years and years of specialist training, and an understanding that is increasingly more radically separated from common sense. As far as quantum physics is concerned, perhaps what is required is a logic different not only to Aristotle's but also to Frege's and Russell's, and Brouwer's. And the Leibnizian dream of transforming thought into calculus shattered on the theorems of Gödel. Modernity, that opened with the Kantian distinction between analytic and synthetic truths, closes on Quine's corrosive criticism of this distinction and on the dissolution of "scientific method" first used by Kuhn and then Feyerabend.

Regardless of these profound theoretical flutterings, man's body has continued to distance itself from the "state of nature," enjoying and enduring its artificiality. And fulfilling, in his new cyborg condition, the old dream of the shamans and mystics: to leave oneself. On the Siberian steppes or in a Rimini discotheque, loaded with heavy metal and glittering spangles, it matters little.

# God's Still Unconscious Intentions

It might seem that the undeniably widening gap of experience (albeit simulated, vicarious, "virtual") allowed modern and late-modern man by technological advancement has nothing to do with the modification of the relation between possible and impossible. But the possible appears to be an evanescent and ambiguous concept, ever since Aristotle:[88] how does one establish a secure criterion of demarcation between possible and impossible, if not by empirically controlling that which, amidst everything considered, has effectively been achieved? But the moment in which an objective, a process, an event are realized, they cease to be purely possible: they are already real, effectual. And the "possible" therefore appears to dissolve into the real. In effect, Aristotle, in discussing the passage from power to action, seems to perceive "impossibility" to be logical impossibility, considering the number of times he falls back on the example of the diagonal of the square, and seems instead to consider "possible," on the operative level anyway, as a relatively extensive concept, and too liberal at that.[89] However, putting logical aporia aside (for now), it is evident that in common thought the notion of what is possible and what is not possible to do (in the operative sense, not the ethical) is dependent on the technical patrimony available at a determinate moment. It is also clear that the idea of "possibility" is linked to that of a "project:" what doesn't exist is still possible, provided there exists a will to realize it. In this case the

---

88     "'Possible,' then, means in one sense, as we have said, that which is not necessarily a lie; in another, that which is true; and in another, that which may be true." Aristotle, *Metaphysics* 5.1019b.

89     "[I]t is impossible that the diagonal of a square should be commensurable with the sides, because such a thing is a lie, whose contrary is not only true but inevitable. Hence that it is commensurable is not only a lie but necessarily a lie. And the contrary of the impossible, i.e. the possible, is when the contrary is not necessarily a lie." Ibid. Besides: "Now if, as we have said, that is possible which does not involve an impossibility, obviously it cannot be true to say that so-and-so is possible, but will not be, this view entirely loses sight of the instances of impossibility." Aristotle, *Metaphysics* 9.1047b.

 ethical concerns are more than present. At least this is the point of view of one of the twentieth century's most decisive "possibilistes", Robert Musil:

> But if there is a sense of reality, and no one will doubt that it has its justifications for existing, then there must also be something we can call a sense of possibility. Whoever has it does not say, for instance: Here this or that has happened, will happen, must happen; but he invents: Here this or that might, could, or ought to happen. If he is told that something is the way it is, he will think: Well, it could probably just as well be otherwise. [...] Such fools are also called idealists by those who wish to praise them. But all this clearly applies only to their weak subspecies, those who cannot comprehend reality or who, in their melancholic condition, avoid it. These are people in whom the lack of a sense of reality is a real deficiency. But the possible includes not only the fantasies of people with weak nerves but also the as yet unwakened intentions of God. A possible experience or truth is not the same as an actual experience or truth minus its "reality value" but has – according to its partisans, at least – something quite divine about it, a fire, a soaring, a readiness to build and a conscious utopianism that does not shrink from reality but sees it as a project, something yet to be invented. After all, the earth is not that old, and was apparently never so ready as now to give birth to its full potential.[90]

Who could doubt that the call to consider reality as an invention, and not as something given once and for all, isn't one of the constants of twentieth century thought and action? Didn't Raymond Roussel suggest bending reality to fit the project (or to the paranoia of dreams) with an erratic and atypical use of science

90   Robert Musil, *The Man Without Qualities*.

and technology, subordinate to the logic of a play on words?[91]  Didn't the pyrotechnics of Dadaism insist on suspending life in order to hand the keys of reality's castle to the allied forces of nonsense, irrationality and sarcasm? Didn't the Surrealists make a desperate attempt to have a never-seen-before but potentially already present heterogeneity rise up from the slums of daily life, and have subconscious automatisms emerge to create a new "common sense" unadulterated by blinding habit? But we must not forget that all this would not have been possible if the Earth's damned had not decided their mother's womb was not only not blessed, but was also decidedly cursed, and if they hadn't made numerous attempts through the century to bless it their own way: by attacking the sky and, if possible, plundering it. Their repeated defeats during the twenties and thirties, and again in the sixties and seventies, in no way signified the condemnation of their "utopian awareness:" they reveal, certainly, the limits of the theoretical and operative tools of the workers' movement from its birth to the present day, and the uselessness, or rather the damage, of committing to every type of historical philosophy, the only result of which being to create a superfetation of organizational procedures, that (pending palingenesis, as desired as it is impossible) easily develops into useful elements of man-agement of that reality that they should have surpassed. But the fact that the only "accomplishments by Utopia" over recent years can be attributed to technology is simply an illuminating paradox that signals a vitality perhaps unexpected by capitalism, but doesn't authorize it to declare the contradictions extinct, or the story "finished."

I feel that Musil's quote above signals however the reversal of a traditional and well-rooted prejudice in Western culture that finds in Aristotle its first great expression: the devaluation of the pos-sible, of the potential, with respect to the actual, the devaluation

---

91    See the posthumous *Comment j'ai écrit certains des mes livres* [How I wrote some of my books].

of "God's intentions" still dormant with respect to those that have been realized, that have become "actual." In Aristotle, as in all classical Greek culture, this devaluation should probably be connected to the fear of *apeiron*, in other words the infinite or unlimited, of what has no boundaries, "in the sense of the untraversable."[92] Starting from the radical acknowledgement of the finiteness of the human condition and of human means, Greek philosophy advises caution in consciously accepting this limitedness; this pre-eminence given to the principle of reality, that touches on every western culture at least until the identification between real and rational worked by Hegel, constitutes however a possibly excessive limitation for the history of a species that makes this very access to possibility its peculiarity and its principle condition of survival.

Naturally, history is littered with passages from the potential to the actual, but also, as previously mentioned, with obstinate and generous attempts by subjectivity to bring some still unfulfilled plan of God to light. The last attempt, made during the previous century, was to overcome capitalism thanks to the development of a "natural" antagonist to capital, natural because it was generated within the growth process of capital itself: the proletariat. In this sense it certainly wasn't Marx who failed, but Marxism; or rather some of the Marxisms that developed starting from the gigantic work by Trier's philosopher, that unfortunately represented, at the level of society, the near totality of the heritage of that philosophy. It is evident that only the most short-sighted or the most deeply prejudiced had to wait until 1989 before being aware of that failure, when it was already quite clear with the defeat of the U.S.'s revolutionary trade-unionism

92 Aristotle, *Metaphysics* 11.1066b, that continues: "Again, how can the infinite exist independently unless number and magnitude, of which infinity is an attribute, also exist independently? And further, if the infinite is accidental, it cannot, qua infinite, be an element of things; just as the invisible is not an element of speech, although sound is invisible. It is clear also that the infinite cannot exist actually."

between the end of the twenties and start of the thirties, the 
despotic establishment of so-called "socialism" in the USSR after
1926, and then in Spain in 1936, and so on. This Marxism was a
failure not because it did not get us out of God's particular configuration called capitalism, but on the contrary it appears to
have strengthened it, building an illusory alternative made up
of a system of states proclaiming themselves "non-capitalist,"
but who in reality were a variation of an even more oppressive
and dictatorial capitalism. And after 1989, capitalism, profoundly
transformed by those cycles of workers' struggles that for more
than twenty years challenged and maligned it, today appears, in
its post-Fordist version, as the planetary victor, the only horizon
possible and therefore the scourge of every possibility ever
written within its own boundaries.

Possibility's opportunity appeared to come, paradoxically, from
another direction. In the second half of the twentieth century, a
somewhat utopian dimension appears to have surfaced not in the
realm of politics—increasingly shackled by its own mechanisms,
its ideals discredited, prisoner of that moral autonomy it had
once proudly claimed, from Machiavelli onwards, and throughout
the modern era—but directly in the field of technology. It is
the advent of digital technologies that appears to suddenly
open what can literally be defined as an "era of the possible," a
redefinition of that same principle of reality; digital simulation
can exit the purely mental environment and speak directly to
man's senses, and thus "make a possible world." The paradox is
not only in the sudden autonomy of a dimension (technology)
that Western thought had always considered ancillary and subordinate to more spiritual or theoretical or cognitive dimensions,
but also in a change of the paradigms of those same tools
fundamental to technology, in the passage from analogical to
digital. The multiplication of the possibilities and the expansion
of virtual spheres, and the accelerated step from virtual to actual
(or the difficulty in detecting stable borders between reality and
imaginary), derive in fact from a process that would instead look

**144**   initially like a terrible impoverishment of reality, the process of digitalization, a process in which the symbolic tools necessary not only to represent the world, but to rebuild it, or to build new ones, are drastically reduced to a combination of just two elements, conventionally the 0 and the 1. The fact that the power of calculation is linked to the humble tool of the discrete, and not to the superb conceptual constructions of the continuum, has been known for some time. What is new is that the advent of the computer, with its explosive increase in the power of calculation, has made it possible to compute any problem, a huge leap forward from using nothing but the human sensorial system. The "millions of colors" present in our computer's palette are way out of reach of even our most perceptive capabilities, and yet they are the indispensable condition for that "realism" of images and virtual worlds, the consequence of which is (another paradox!) what many judge to be the radical irrealism that surrounds us.

## Possibility and Necessity

The advent of the digital era was not unexpected. In some ways, the entire twentieth century had prepared for it. On a theoretical plane, the digital age is the child of that "revenge" of the discrete over the continuum; one that was produced in the logical reflection on mathematics between the end of the nineteenth century and the first decades of the twentieth. From the establishment of the theory of real numbers and the foundation of set theory by Greg Cantor after 1870, the question of the "principles of mathematics" became one of that discipline's fundamental lines of research. Whether it dealt with Peano axioms, Hilbert's space, or Frege and Russell's still more ambitious and radical objective logistics, their aim being to reduce all mathematics to a question of logic, at the start of the twentieth century no one could have denied the importance of natural numbers (the discrete) for the foundation of the principle instrument of mathematical analysis, namely real numbers (the continuum).

It is true that from the theoretical point of view this revenge 
creates more problems than it solves.[93] In 1902, Russell, reflecting
on the logical system explained in Frege's *Arithmetic Principles*,
pointed out, with the famous antinomy that bears his name, that
the principle of comprehension was too extensive, too powerful,
and his application to the classes of all classes led to a contradiction (regarding, in his case, the class of all classes that do not
contain themselves as an element); Russell demonstrated that
his antinomy was analogous to others that had emerged in the
nineteenth century and others even older, already known to the
Megarians and the Stoics, like that of the liar, otherwise known
as Epimenides the Cretan (Epimenides of Knossos, the land
where everyone lies, affirms: "I lie"). According to Russell, they
were all bound to self-reference, in other words to the difficulty
of defining their own communes to all the members of a certain
class by referring to the totality of the class itself. In short, the
Greeks' *apeiron* came back to haunt the philosophers' dreams.
Then in 1931, Gödel's famous treatise "On formally indescribable
propositions of *Principia Mathematica* and related systems
I"[94] administered the coup de grâce to the formal theory and
numbers programs, and to Hilbert's program in particular, demonstrating not only the synthetic incompleteness of arithmetic,
but more generally the impossibility of demonstrating the consistency of a logical system within the system itself (if the latter
is powerful enough to formulate the arithmetic): to escape the
swamp, Baron Münchhausen cannot extract himself from it by
pulling on his own ponytail.

But the research, naturally, doesn't stop because of the impossibility of a formal demonstration of coherency. And neither does
the practice allow itself to be halted by the subtleties of theory.
Calculation technologies use all the theoretical instrumentation

93    See William C. Kneale and Martha Kneale, *The Development of Logic* (Oxford
      and New York, Oxford University Press, 1962).
94    Kurt Gödel, *Collected Works. Volume 1, 1929–1936* (Oxford and New York:
      Oxford University Press, 1986).

 of the extraordinary period that opened up for formal logic, but without being paralyzed by the irrefutable, by Hercules' pillars that Gödel defined in theory. *Apeiron* does not frighten the English technicians who during the Second World War succeed in breaking German codes, thus giving rise to the practical realization of that "universal machine", the calculations of which Turing had already formulated a theory in 1936. At the start of the fifties, von Neumann's computer allows the discrete to enjoy further revenge over the continuum, in a manner somewhat different from that dreamed of by Hilbert and Frege, but just as powerful, if not more so. And so a technology apparently based on a reduction of possibilities (everything is reducible to 0 or 1, without exception) succeeds instead, via the combinatory power of its applications, to expand the horizon of possibilities in a way never seen before, obliquely reviving and fulfilling (in a distorted and contorted way, sometimes akin to a nightmare) dreams that were once those of the artistic avant-garde, of linguistic and literary experimentation, and even of political and social opposition. Technology accomplished the only successful revolution of the twentieth century, which perhaps suggests that we should use the word "revolution" more sparingly.

I can't help but suspect that there is some underground link, which a story on scientific and philosophical thought of a materialistic nature should investigate, between a cultural and historical mood that rendered possible the birth of informatics, and the discussion on the difference between analytical and synthetic truth that took place in the first half of the twentieth century and is still with us today, but to which Willard van Orman Quine strongly railed, his attack one of the most severe against the concept of necessity, exactly fifty years ago. Like the term "possibility", "necessity" is also a word that suffers from a dangerous semantic indeterminacy that didn't stop it from becoming, over the centuries, a pivotal concept of philosophy. For Aristotle two most "philosophical" meanings of the term "necessary" ("Furthermore, we say that anything which cannot be otherwise in a given situation is necessary"[95]; and "Again, demonstration is a "necessary" thing, because a thing cannot be otherwise if the demonstration has been absolute.") [96] proceeds from the most usual meanings of the term: necessity as "[t]hat without which, as a concomitant condition, life is impossible; e.g. respiration and food are necessary for an animal" and necessity as in coercion, like "something inexorable; for it is opposed to motion which is in accordance with purpose and calculation."[97] Paradoxically, Voltaire recognizes the contingent character of necessity in the sense that "what is necessary for one man to live, … from the moment that what is necessary for one man is not always necessary to the other; rice is necessary to an Indian, meat is necessary to an Englishman," and concentrates more on "what is necessary to all men", before concluding with a negative conception of necessity: "I clearly recognize what is false, and know little about what is true."[98]

Necessity, from Kant onwards and especially in the twentieth century, within the sphere of logical empiricism, was meant as logical necessity, and necessary truths were identified with analytical truths, assertions that say nothing about the world, that have no empiric content, only linguistic. Empirical truths, with regard to our knowledge of the world, are instead synthetic assertions that express contingent truths, going back to Leibniz's terminology, they are true only in some of the "possible worlds" (including ours for sure), not in all of them. The necessary truths, on the other hand, must be so in every possible way. The philosophical program of logical empiricism (Rudolf Carnap's, for example) assumes this distinction, since it provides philosophy with the task of building a solid "logical syntax of the language", leaving the task of broadening our knowledge of the world to empiric science. But in 1951, Quine, the forty-year-old American


95   Aristotle, *Metaphysics* ? [trans. Robert Booth].
96   Aristotle, *Metaphysics* 5.1015b.
97   Ibid., 5.1015a.
98   Voltaire, *Dictionnaire Philosophique* (1764).

philosopher who had worked with Carnap, in the essay *"Two Dogmas of Empiricism"*[99] took the ideas of logical positivism in an unexpected direction. Sharing the idea that a line of demarcation between facts and language may only be drawn when analyzing linguistic behavior, Quine pointed out that within the language it is impossible—if not based upon extralinguistic assumptions and therefore "unverifiable" with language itself—to say where the reference to empiric reality ends and where the linguistic treatment of the empiric content begins. Therefore, he concluded, it needs to recognize that there is no line between analytical and synthetic affirmations, and that the exigency to draw such a line is "a non-empirical dogma of the empiricists, but a metaphysical article of faith."

Putnam, while discussing the proposal to introduce a "quantum logic" that allows the "empiric facts" of quantum mechanics to be handled without paradoxes, commented: "The laws of logic, on this perspective, are as empirical as the laws of geometry, only more abstract and better protected. Logic is the last thing we shall everrevise, on Quine's view, but it is not immune from revision."[100] Quine did not mean to abandon the notion of necessity completely, but he weakened it considerably, turning it into a type of pragmatic requisite (these statements are "necessary" because, without them, the "cost" to the system they belong to would be far too great). To close this brief and fragmentary review of the "revenge of the possible" during the twentieth century, one must take note of how the attempt to save the

99    Willard van Orman Quine, *"Two Dogmas of Empiricism,"* in *The Philosophical Review* 60, no. 1 (1951): 20–43. For the discussion that took place of the following decades on the problem established by Quine see also Hilary Putnam, *Mind, Language and Reality: Philosophical Papers, vol. 2* (Cambridge: Cambridge University Press, 1975).

100    Hilary Putnam, "Possibility and Necessity," in *Realism and Reason: Philosophical Papers*, vol. 3 (Cambridge: Cambridge University Press, 1983), 51. It is worth noting the analogy of Quine's positions with regard to the criticism of empirical logic in the thirties by Popper, and then with the developments of "post-Popper" epistemology.

notion of necessity from twentieth-century modal logic (and from Kripke in particular) went through the notion of possibility: the necessary assertions, from this point of view, would be valid in all possible worlds. Without arguing the solidity of this notion of necessity, and without entering into the delicate question of the definition of "possible worlds" (a concept that has become far more sophisticated since the first formulations by Leibniz), it is evident that in this way necessity is, somehow, no longer a "primitive" modal category, because the role of the fundamental modal notion shifts over to the concept of possibility.

## To Leave Oneself

The cyborg is one of the more radical and astonishing "possibles" that have emerged from the contemporary magma; here, we have tried to show that it is one of its key figures. However, the cyborg is not a definitive, fully established figure, it is more a process, one of the many processes of hybridism characterizing late modernity: physical and cultural, material and communicative hybridism between different species, between living and non-living, between organic and inorganic, and thus between man and machine. The process to artificialize the body that, as we have seen, is innate to the process of human evolution, has, in the last decades, registered such an acceleration that one is led to suspect that there has been a real surge of quality, a passage (some might say) from human to *posthuman*.

Naturally, the hybrid is not an invention of modernity, nor of late modernity. On the contrary, we could almost say that today's proliferation of hybrids is no more than the resurgence of a distant age largely populated by these beings, the time of myth, and to remain more in touch with our cultural roots, namely Greek mythology. But beyond the "raw material," the components of this figure (animal or machine), there exists a substantial difference between the Greek hybrid and its contemporary counterpart that is underlined by the etymology of the name.

**150**  In fact, the root of "hybrid" comes from the Greek *hýbris*, that is insolence, arrogance, excess, challenge; to put it simply, like that of Capaneus at the walls of Thebes, as described by Dante as well. And against whom is the insolence of the hybrid, of arrogance, intended? In the case of the "mixed" figures, of the proud mix of man-animal, it is directed against the order of the cosmos that established the separation between men and gods, between one species of animal and another. The centaur and the chimera, with the arrogant composition of their bodies, challenge this order, want to escape *Ananke's* dominion, the steely necessity to which even the other gods must bow. They are figures that take us back to primordial chaos, to the intolerable immoderation of a still disorderly world. In some way, they too are connected to the *apeiron*, to infinite wickedness. And are thus inevitably destined to lose.

In the era of possibility, Ananke's grip is no longer so strong. The contemporary hybrids walk the streets of New York and Rome, of Los Angeles and London, without fear of harassment. Of course, particularly "scandalous" biological-cultural hybrids, like sexual hybrids on the transgender road, are still vulnerable to reproach, if not disgust, from the more traditionalist, who are probably still in the majority in industrial and post-industrial urban cultures. But there is a place for them too, seeing that they perform a role in the underground economy of transgression, reproached by the media and tolerated in private. So contemporary hybrids have somehow won the right to citizenship, no matter how formal. Their existence is more or less guaranteed by the repressive tolerance that pervades late capitalism. The possibility, even the most "monstrous" and perverse, now has a degree more legitimacy with respect to the past. Naturally, all this comes at a price: social irrelevancy. If deviance, even hybrid deviance, loses its "oppositional" nature in order to embrace the more bourgeois and modest practice of "transgression", it is tolerated and even encouraged by managers who run the various outlets of entertainment, from discotheques to sex shops; in some measure, transgression is integrated into the broader  mechanisms of social reproduction, precisely because it doesn't interfere with the more profound workings of the social machine as such.

Is the contemporary hybrid, therefore, no longer capable of challenging society, of standing out, of causing cracks in the cosmos? One should not be too sure. The hybridism between man and technology that takes place in the cyborg produces a truly new situation, heralds an undeniable discontinuity in the process of artificiality. Technology now penetrates the skin at every level and with every possible modality, as much in the electro-mechanical cyborg as in the genetic one. In both these extreme cases, and in their every conceivable intermediate gradation, a displacement between internal and external is produced, one that works on the conditions and modalities of experience. The cyborg is a figure that leaves itself, much like a religious mystic or devotee of religious tradition, but in a literal and physical manner, not only mentally and imaginatively. Its ecstasy (or *ekstasis*, to be outside oneself, to leave one's body) is no longer an exceptional and extraordinary experience, it is a daily condition, permanent, despite being reversible in some ways. This is why its experience cannot be the same as the traditional man. This, not something else, denotes the posthuman perspective: the cyborg lives with its brain outside its head and its nerves outside its skin, to quote McLuhan, and no longer knows the meaning of "inner" with respect to "outer," and lives in a state of continual ecstasy.

Undoubtedly, all this creates a state of destabilization, new contradictions between individual and collective. It seems to me there are two principles. The first regards the cultural processes of humanization. The presence of a stable frontier between internal and external, as far as the body is concerned, has always been one of the stronger mechanisms of cultural stabilization. In societies lacking the art of writing, that frontier—the skin—could and should only be passed through at particular moments, like the initiation ceremony, with a highly visible artificiality of the body involving lacerations, wounds, insertion of various objects, all symbols of the "humanization" of the body, that only then could, once the difference with the animal's body had been affirmed, recover and reaffirm one's place in the cosmic order on the basis of this difference. But when the line between the body's interior and exterior is passed through every time, as much with surgery as with piercing, this act might not lose its traumatic effect (plastic surgery, like the application of a pacemaker, is painful nonetheless), but it definitely loses its cultural nature. The cyborg cannot affirm its "humanity" once and for all (or the equivalent of humanity for a cyborg of that sort), it has to continuously renegotiate it socially: its life becomes a permanent ritual of initiation, a journey constantly renewed by a mobile, fluctuating frontier. This, I believe, is the characteristic that convinced Donna Haraway to make it the central figure of her process of liberation.

The second contradiction concerns appropriation procedures and the use of technology. The individual dimension has become preponderant in the new information and communication technologies. The consumption of products of the imaginary, in particular, has shifted unequivocally from the collective rites and, in some measure, from the film community to the more familiar world of television, and to those of the drastically individualized computer. Nonetheless, the telematics networks develop new forms of communication, of contacts between different subjectivities that escape the uniformity of television, to the reduction of the subject to a passive receptor of messages conceived, packaged and distributed centrally. Almost naturally, the networks evoke the image of a "collective intelligence".
The prevalent form that this collective intelligence currently assumes is for the moment that of financial instruments of economic globalization, of business-to-business contacts that in a few nanoseconds decide the destiny of exchange rates, stock markets, the economies of entire nations. All this has little to do with the angelic intelligence evoked by the telematics optimism

of Pierre Lévy. Once again the collective nature of the networks  appears to rise up against the individual like a new version of the state's alienating power, a monument to impersonality, to the control of the masses and the formalism of "dead" labor against pulsating individuality, the autonomy and existential wealth of "living" labor. However, the word "labor" has over the past twenty years lost much of its significance, rendering its use very difficult when describing such dissimilar realities like Fordist labor and post-Fordist labor. This is another, even more insidious term for "cyborg ecstasy." Can the collective power of the networks become a general intellect aimed to build up liberation practices or is it destined to reproduce mechanisms of alienation and of other-directed means disguised as individual choice? How can I "re-enter myself" after leaving myself, how can I recover the intelligent, emotional and affective wealth that I helped to construct in the exteriorization phase, having left my own dimension? How can I conserve and enrich my body after temporarily abandoning it to the networks, after having experimented with sophisticated technological, but seemingly immaterial, versions of the same? How can I return home if, instead of *one* home, I have numerous homes, virtual dwellings of my hybrid and telematic existence? These questions will stay with us for a long time, well into the opening century of the new millennium.

# POSTSCRIPT

## [ 1 0 ]

# From the Cyborg to the Posthuman

The term "posthuman" gained the attention of the cultural media
with the "Post Human" exhibition organized by merchant and
critic Jeffrey Deitch of Lausanne's FAE Musée d'Art Contemporian
in June 1992, before being housed over the following years at
Turin's Castello di Rivoli and other European contemporary art
museums and institutions. Taking another look at it today, the
exhibition appears far less "posthuman" than one might expect.
The star of the exhibition was Jeff Koons, whose work, created
during his marriage to Cicciolina, Deitch preferred to describe
as posthuman, in so far as the highly realistic sculptures of the
couple's union or the reproductions of superheroes seemed to
be more in line with cheap pop art or frenzied name-dropping.
Not even the exhibition works of Mike Kelley, Charles Ray,
Paul McCarthy, Kiki Smith, Janine Antoni and others showed
any particular tendency towards theriomorphic or mechanical
hybridism, as already seen in the works of Stelarc or Orlan.
However, the exhibition not only enjoyed significant success,
it also provoked discussion and reflection that concurred with

 the problems mentioned by Deitch in the catalog's introductory remarks.

In this prologue, Deitch focused on the new possibilities offered by biotechnology in order to look into various aspects of our body and personality: "There is a growing sense that we should take control over our bodies and our social circumstances rather than just accepting what we inherited."[101] The chance to intervene in the genetic patrimony to ensure us and our descendants particular physical, mental and behavioral traits, led Deitch to affirm that we are going from a Darwinian evolution, or "natural evolution", to an "artificial evolution". Broadly speaking, to rebuild the conceptual history of Western modernity from the point of view of its own models of self-construction (even when assisted by the history of art), Deitch gives particular significance to 1968 ("when the culture of modernism reached both its culmination and its collapse") and the importance of feminism. The critic argued that the new ways of the organization of personality involved as a consequence the annulment of privileged models of self from the point of view of "fair play" or of the truth. The "collapse of absolutes" applied not only to personality models, but to political and social models as well: the collapse of communism in the Soviet Union, the puncture of Japan's bubble economy, and the crisis of the modern corporation's social functions were more examples of this final aspect of the process.

What is interesting to note is that Deitch made a point of underlining the connection between these fragmented and multiple models of self and the debilitation of rationality but the push towards irrationalism came about without scandal, and the condemnation of the negative collateral effects of the process was expressed with relative coldness:

101   Jeffrey Deitch, "Post Human Exhibit Catalog Essay 1992–93", http://www.artic.edu/~pcarroll/PostHuman.html.

The structure of thinking is changing, and it appears that the quality of thinking is changing as well. Patterns of thinking are becoming less rational. With the collapse of many of the modern era's hierarchical belief systems, and their replacement by multifaceted alternatives, people are moving away from hierarchically structured rational thinking to a more perceptual. less structured outlook and a more irrational mode of thought. An irrational outlook in fact might be a more appropriate approach to a world that seems to have outgrown its modern utopian faith in rational solutions. This feeling of irrationality is furthered by the sense that the explosive new technologies may also be unleashing some explosive new pathologies. We are experiencing a surge of seemingly untamable viruses: biological, social, environmental, and computer viruses as well. There is a sense that we are advancing but not progressing, mired in a swirl of unexpected side effects that have undermined our belief in a rational order and moved us closer to embracing an irrational model of the world.[102]

In other words, the idea that Deitch conveyed was sufficiently optimistic: it was the conviction that the storm of post-modern (of which the posthuman represented an ulterior articulation and in-depth analysis) was no more than the premise for a successive, imminent theoretical and practical rearrangement of the relationship between man and the world: "The modern era might be characterized as a period of the discovery of self. Our current post-modern era can be characterized as a transitional period of the disintegration of self. Perhaps the coming "post-human" period will be characterized by the reconstruction of self.[103]

Despite the scarce sympathy (or scarce interest) for the more truly scientific thematics, those ideas were, however, also the result of a seemingly endless debate developed in the previous

102   Ibid.
103   Ibid.

 decade on scientific-technological research. Since the eighties, the most radical and extreme positions have emerged in the field of AI, like those of Eric Drexler (*Engines of Creation*, 1986) and Hans Moravec (*Mind Children*, 1988), visionary scientists convinced that the new frontiers of research would soon have allowed individuals to control and modify their own morphology. The first struggled to foresee revolutionary developments in nanotechnology, meant to supply nanorobot agents at an atomic and molecular level, as much to construct apparatuses and automatic machines so as to intervene in the capillary workings of the human body (the so-called "assemblers", a line of research that until now does not appear to have had much success),[104] the second, director of the Mobile Robot Laboratory at Carnegie Mellon University at the time, boldly announced that within a short period of time "the human race (would be) swept away by tide of cultural changes, usurped by its own artificial progeny."[105] In fact, Moravec predicted that in less than fifty years (about 2030), research would be capable of producing robots at least as intelligent as humans, and that science and technology would permit a human being's mental capacity to be transferred to a machine (a sort of backup or download of the human brain to a machine; "mind uploading" the author called it). In one way or another, willy-nilly, the human race would step aside in favor of its mechanical or, more likely, its organic-mechanical heirs. In their own different way, both Drexler and Moravec brought up man's age-old dream of immortality.

We certainly couldn't have done without someone reprising this old dream. Though perhaps not in such an apocalyptical fashion. The year in which Moravec's book was published (1988) coincided with the release of *Extropy Magazine's* first edition, run by Max More and Tom Morrow. The Extropy Institute was founded four

---

104 K. Eric Drexler, *Engines of Creation: The coming era of Nanotechnology* (New York: Anchor Press/Doubleday, 1986).

105 Hans Moravec, *Mind Children: The Future of Robot and Human Intelligence* (Cambridge, MA: Harvard University Press, 1988), 2.

years later in 1992.[106] The component "extropic" of the transhumanist movement was born, in the wake of ideas by Fereidoun M. Esfandiary, a sociologist-futurologist of New York's New School for Social Research. In 1973, he published *UpWingers: A Futurist Manifesto*, predicting an era of continuous technological progress until the conquest of immortality.[107] The year 1998 saw instead the birth of the World Transhumanist Association,[108] another component of this line of thought, thanks to Nick Bostrom and David Pearce. The transhumanist movement, in all its facets, takes the posthuman concept very seriously. For transhumanists, hybridity with technology is rapidly turning human beings into a totally new biological species, placing natural evolution alongside a "cultural evolution". "What is a posthuman?" is one of the FAQs on the Extropic site, and the answer is: "A posthuman is a human descendent who has been augmented to such a degree as to be no longer a human". It is even clearer on the American site:

> "Posthuman" is a term used by transhumanists to refer to what humans could become if we succeed in using technology to remove the limitations of the human condition. No one can be certain exactly what posthumans would be like (there may be many differing types, and they may continuing changing) but we can understand the term by contrasting it with "human": Posthumans would be those who have overcome the biological, neurological, and psychological constraints built into humans by the evolutionary process. Posthumans would have a far greater ability to reconfigure and sculpt their physical form and function;



---

106   http://www.extropy.org. The Extropy Institute was closed in 2006. The web site works as the archive of this transhumanist component, while the mailing list (on the same site) remains active.

107   In acknowledging his conviction, Esfiandiary later changed his name to FM-2030 to indicate that his hundredth birthday would be in 2030. Unfortunately, FM-2030 died of pancreatic cancer in 2000. His body is still kept in cryogenic suspension until technology might perhaps bring him back to life. http://en.wikipedia.org/wiki/FM-2030.

108   http://transhumanism.org.

they would have an expanded range of refined emotional responses, and would possess intellectual and perceptual abilities enhanced beyond the purely human range. Posthumans would not be subject to biological aging or degeneration.[109]

The transhumanists' insistence on improving their morphology and physical appearance (like their scrupulous attention to the managerial aspects of all their intellectual and organizational activities) is a sign of their strong roots in North American culture. Max Moore, who is of English origin, does not ignore the connections of his futuristic platform with the utopic European tradition, but declines it in an unequivocally "reasonable" form, taking great care to distance himself from every banally ufological, science fiction aspect, and from every reference to contingent political debate. The liberalism of the transhumanists is a moderate liberalism, just as their utopia is one that treads carefully and refuses every eschatological perspective:

> It would be unrealistic to expect posthumans to be "perfect" by our standards. What we *can* reasonably say is that posthumans would have greater *potential* for good or bad, just as humans have greater potential than other primate species.[110]

To be convinced of this, one simply has to check the titles of the seven "Principles of Extropy"[111]: perpetual progress, self-transformation, practical optimism, intelligent technology, open society (information and democracy), self-direction, rational thinking. Nevertheless, the utopic tension of transhumanist thought is beyond question, just like its syncretic ambitions to reconnect the cul-de-sacs of Western thought to the main highway of scientific and technological progress. "We have achieved two of the three alchemists' dreams," More writes in *On Becoming Posthuman*. "We

109  http://www.extropy.org/faq.htm.
110  Ibid.
111  http://www.extropy.org/principles.htm.

have transmuted the elements and learned to fly. Immortality is 
next."

The transhuman, in keeping with his name, looks upon himself "as a transitional stage between our animal heritage and our posthuman future."[112] In this setting, even experimenting with new expressive and communicative forms is envisaged.

> Transhumanist Artists embrace the creative innovations of transhumanity.
> We are ardent activists in pursuing infinite transformation, overcoming death and exploring the universe.[113]

But the transhumanists naturally give their all when it comes to short/medium term forecasts: essentially, they remain futurologists seduced by the principles of a strong AI, and firmly convinced of the postulates that govern this discipline (firstly, the algorithmic nature of intelligence and therefore its dependence on biological support, namely from the body). In this sense, one of the more interesting and paradigmatic characters in this movement is Ray Kurzwell, futurologist and successful inventor, as well as brilliant propagator of the quality improvement we expect in the near future.

Having graduated in Computer Science and Literature from MIT in 1970, Kurzweil has a notable career as a technologist and entrepreneur, especially in the field of optical character recognition (OCR), in music synthesizers and in technologies for the arts in general.[114] Kurzweil's ideas on the future of humanity are presented in three books: *The Age of Intelligent Machines,*

---

112  Ibd.

113  "Transhumanist Art Statement", http://www.transhumanist.biz/trans-humanistartsmanifesto. This was edited by Natasha Vita-More (www.natasha.cc) in 1982 and revised in 2003. "Transhumanist Art Statement" is not very rich, and consists of a few performances and some videos made in the eighties and nineties predominantly by Natasha Vita-More herself.

114  http://en.wikipedia.org/wiki/Ray_Kurzweil.

**164** *The Age of Spiritual Machines* and *The Singularity is Near*.[115] The concept of "technological singularity" (the term is borrowed from mathematics and physics) was first used in 1983 by science fiction writer Vernon Vinge in the magazine *Omni*, based on ideas by statistician I. J. Good during the mid-sixties.[116] Elaborated by Kurzweil, the term indicates a highly rapid (but not discontinuous) rise in AI and its fusion with human intelligence towards the middle of the twenty-first century (the author dates it 2045). Kurzweil explained in an interview:

> Within a quarter century, nonbiological intelligence will match the range and subtlety of human intelligence. It will then soar past it because of the continuing acceleration of information-based technologies, as well as the ability of machines to instantly share their knowledge. Intelligent nanorobots will be deeply integrated in our bodies, our brains, and our environment, overcoming pollution and poverty, providing vastly extended longevity, full-immersion virtual reality incorporating all of the senses (like "The Matrix"), "experience beaming" (like "Being John Malkovich"), and vastly enhanced human intelligence. The result will be an intimate merger between the technology-creating species and the technological evolutionary process it spawned. [...] [After which] nonbiological intelligence will have access to its own design and will be able to improve itself in an increasingly rapid redesign cycle. We'll get to a point where technical progress will be so fast that unenhanced human intelligence will be unable to follow it. That will mark the Singularity.[117]


115 *The Age of Intelligent Machines* (New York: Viking, 1990); *The Age of Spiritual Machines: When Computers Exceed Human Intelligence* (New York: Viking, 1998); *The Singularity is Near: When Humans Transcend Biology* (New York: Viking, 2005).

116 http://en.wikipedia.org/wiki/Technological_singularity.

117 http://www.singularity.com/qanda.html

Kurzweil pursues and generalizes Moore's law on technological 
acceleration, maintaining that the passage from a linear change
or polynomial tax to an exponential one (what he calls the "law
of accelerated returns") induces such a situation that we can
no longer use traditional categories to interpret "the cycle of
human life, including death itself. Understanding the Singularity
will alter our perspective on the significance of our past and the
ramifications for our future. To truly understand it inherently
changes one's view of life in general and one's own particular
life."[118] The change that he outlines from here to the middle of
the twenty-first century (in a little less than forty years) includes
radical transformations due to the combination of the three great
sectors of technological innovation: genetics, nanotechnology
and robotics. This involves a profound and definitive change
not only in our daily routine but also in the human body, and
overcoming its traditional limits, like aging and death. Like
other transhumanists, Kurzweil considers death to be the great
bogeyman. Except that now we have the means to defeat it:

> In my view, death is a tragedy. It's a tremendous loss of per-
> sonality, skills, knowledge, relationships. We've rationalized
> it as a good thing because that's really been the only
> alternative we've had. But disease, aging, and death are
> problems we are now in a position to overcome.[119]

It is significant, when Kurzweil describes the future, that not only
is technology the prime factor taken into consideration, but that
every reference and debate between human intelligence (and
biological in general) and AI is made exclusively on the basis of
reasonably simple measurable dimensions, typically speed and
the power of calculation or, more in general, the treatment of
information. Not that other dimensions are absent from this discourse, but it all comes down to technological fact. In principle,
transhumanists do not ignore the inherent risks and dangers in

118   Kurzweil, *The Singularity is Near*, 7.
119   http://www.singularity.com/qanda.html.

 the exponential advance of technology, but think that all things considered, the latter together with the problems generates the solutions too. They don't pretend to identify the array of human experience with "solving the problems," but believe that in the final analysis the first is reduced to the second. Therefore, we are faced with radically reductionist thought with regard to human beings, and radical optimism concerning the potential of technology.

Naturally, not everyone looks with the same regard upon the prospect of a growing integration between man and machine, nor the enthusiasm for such a catastrophic and shattering "technological singularity". Others see the cyborg's perspective—given the current conditions of technologies' pervasiveness that render it possible—as a restraint on individual and social freedom, and as a demonstration of violence on the part of the techno-scientific and economic elite who sustain the planet's fortunes. Here is what was said by Jaimie Smith-Windsor, a political science scholar at the University of Victoria in Canada, after seeing her daughter spend months in an incubator following her premature birth in 2003:

> In a sense, all of humanity has become disembodied from the womb. The genesis of a cyborg goes well beyond the physical union of machine with body. The day I gave birth to a cyborg, I began to understand how every human has become a collaboration of mechanic and biological matter. The human condition is mediated by technology. The metanarrative of being cyborg ignores ethical questions. The machine can't ask: What would the world look like without mothers? Or, for that matter, fathers? Technology is, quite literally, beginning to rewire the way we do family, the way we know humanity. The ultimate violence of technology is its ability to generate its own invisibility, to circulate undetected in and through the physical body, to become manifest in the human consciousness as epistemic reality. Conditions of possibility other than becoming cyborg are thus, hidden from

the human condition. Once technology has been internalized and operates upon us through invisible episteme, it becomes the only way of being human. Engaging in a binary relationship with technology is merely one means of engaging with new conditions of possibility for the human condition. However, human/machine symbiosis simultaneously negates the possibility for narrative of "being in the world" and simultaneously forgets all of the moments of differentiation and deferral that work to inform the human essence.[120]

The debate on posthumanism has also started in Italy. In 2005, from January to April, the Faculty of Communication Sciences at University of Rome "La Sapienza", hosted a seminar on this subject that saw the participation of numerous internal and external lecturers, whose speeches were then collected in a book.[121] Another convention was organized in 2007 at the State University of Milan and at the University of Languages and Communication Sciences in Milan.[122] And other initiatives took place at other locations, including the masterclass for Pietro Ingrao's birthday held by Pietro Barcellona at Rome's *Centro per la Riforma dello Stato* (CRS) in 2007, also collected in a book.[123] It was here where Barcellona elaborated on a position of a Marxist matrix opposed and violently critical of the prospect of posthumanism that nonetheless is worth looking at with attention. The starting point was the political crisis and the defeat of the communist movement at the end of the twentieth century:

Tronti is right when he affirms that the end of the communist movement is at the same time the end of politics,

---

120 Jaimie Smith-Windsor, "The Cyborg Mother: A Breached Boundary", *C-Theory* 2/4/2004, http://www.ctheory.net/articles.aspx?id=409#bio

121 Mario Pireddu and Antonio Tursi, eds., *Post-umano. Relazioni tra uomo e tecnologia nella società delle reti* (Milan: Guerini e Associati, 2006).

122 "Post-umano. Percorsi di soggettività attuali," Università degli Studi di Milano, Facoltà di Lettere e Filosofia, Dipartimento di Filosofia / IULM, 22-23/10/2007.

123 Pietro Barcellona, *L'epoca del postumano* (Troina: Citta Aperta, 2007).

understood as man's huge effort to create an autonomous space compared to biological-naturalistic production and reproduction of the species: the aim of the creation of sense, of the individual and collective goals that lend dignity to human action. *If in principle the bourgeois is the natural-biological man, in principle the politician is his antagonist.*

Barcellona defends the modern project with determination, diligence and pride, and identifies his aims with the philosophical assumptions and values of a dualistic and anthropocentric perspective and with the political management of society by the political left. And with these assumptions he sees in the '68 movements (given the reductive label of the "youth protest") the antecedent and embryo of what he considers a catastrophe: "the regression of the individualistic ideal to a form of infantile narcissism, aimed solely at satisfying every need". The posthuman is seen as the turning point that dissolves all dignity and human awareness, that "offers a representation of humanity much closer to that of the primate than to the spiritual longing for a relationship with the divine. The communist crisis signals the end of the humanistic illusion and opens the door to the posthuman scene". The process of the modern subject's dissolution is quickly identified with the transformation of the capitalist economy in the post-Fordist sense and with the abandonment of the dualist mind/body hypothesis:

> Pluralization of subjectivity to extreme singularity, dissemination of the productive cycle to the denial of any territorial relation, criticism of subjectivity's humanistic model founded on the dualism of mind and body; these are the elements of the new constellation.[124]

Barcellona's first misunderstanding is in accepting the bourgeois claim of being a "natural man", of capitalism being a "natural method of production", of the market being a "natural model of

---

124   Ibid., 20–21 [trans. Robert Booth].

human relations." Naturally, not one of these claims is grounded: 
bourgeoisie, capitalism and market are not "natural," they are
historical constructions and therefore contingent, and finally
subject to social change and the logic of conflict—and Barcellona
knows this only too well. But none of it authorizes him to con-
ceive of "authentically human" processes that *transcend* nature
and biology, as they do not authorize a vision of politics and
communism in a post-biological dimension. In this recovery and
"leftist" exasperation with the anthropocentric model there is
a basic misunderstanding: in effect, this upswing is possible
only if one accepts what one claims to criticize, which is the
identification of capitalism with nature, of the bourgeois with the
"human essence". The presumed naturalism of the bourgeoisie
is thus set against the belief in the transcendence of man, whose
only foundation, as we have seen, is no more than a dualist separation between mind and body.

The transcendence of the biological is no more than a spiritual
or idealistic position that pops back in through the window
after being shown the door. What does it mean to call upon
the "ought", "value," to a "principle of validity as opposed to
the immanent normativity of economic progress?" It means
admitting to the fact that when it comes to satisfying survival
needs, in the field of pure "biology," capitalism has already won.
To overcome capitalism one must transcend that field and place
oneself on a higher, more worthy plane—one that overcomes
biology. However, to refuse posthuman in the name of a "return
to human," of a proudly reaffirmed anthropocentrism as the only
possible setting for the production of sense, can only mean an
idealistic refusal of the new conditions of associated life and of
social production, only from whose interior can practical and
experimental research be developed to overcome the existent.

To choose the path of opposition between "communist" finalism
and "naturalist" automatism of the economy means reintroducing
a separation of man from the kingdom of the living which
paradoxically reduces his autonomy. If "philosophy of history and

 philosophy of the subject, from this point of view, coincide within the era of the establishment of modernity's inaugural space," then the criticism of finalism and the recognition of artificiality of every *telos* is at the same time the criticism of the subject and of its claim to separate from its own processes. Barcellona's horror at the "posthuman" perspective coincides paradoxically, in the prior assumptions, with the transhumanists' excitement over the same perspective. Man's separation from biology (feared or desired, it doesn't matter) is possible only if it starts from a fissile conception of human nature, from an essentialism that sees in the human being the possibility of identifying a collection of individualistic, positive and distinctive traits: but every attempt of this type inevitably leads to mistaking a collection of characteristics and determinate historic properties for "human nature," a particular "state of art" that is destined to transform itself through cultural evolvement and mutation. There is no other distinctive trait, no other possible way of describing "human nature" if not by its extreme and variable adaptability, its acceptance of the possible, its relational and hybrid vocation that, starting from an undeniably biological specificity, branches off culturally in the most varied and diverse ways. Essentialism, however disguised, leads inevitably to anthropocentrism and, once again, it is in this context that joyous, naïve technological optimism and dark, pessimistic catastrophism come face to face without recognition.

www.ingramcontent.com/pod-product-compliance
Lightning Source LLC
Chambersburg PA
CBHW020040310726
48970CB00007B/2344